BRIDGE
OF SOULS

BRIDGE
OF SOULS

VICTORIA SCHWAB

SCHOLASTIC

Published in the UK by Scholastic Children's Books, 2021
Euston House, 24 Eversholt Street, London, NW1 1DB, UK
A division of Scholastic Limited.

London – New York – Toronto – Sydney – Auckland
Mexico City – New Delhi – Hong Kong

First published in the US by Scholastic Inc, 2021

ISBN 978 0702 30428 6

A CIP catalogue record for this book is available from the British Library.

Printed by CPI Group (UK) Ltd, Croydon, CR0 4YY
Papers used by Scholastic Children's Books are made
from wood grown in sustainable forests.

1 3 5 7 9 10 8 6 4 2

www.scholastic.co.uk

TO THE KIDS WHO STEP INTO THE DARK, EVEN IF IT SCARES THEM.

"BECAUSE I COULD NOT STOP FOR DEATH - HE KINDLY STOPPED FOR ME-"

~Emily Dickinson

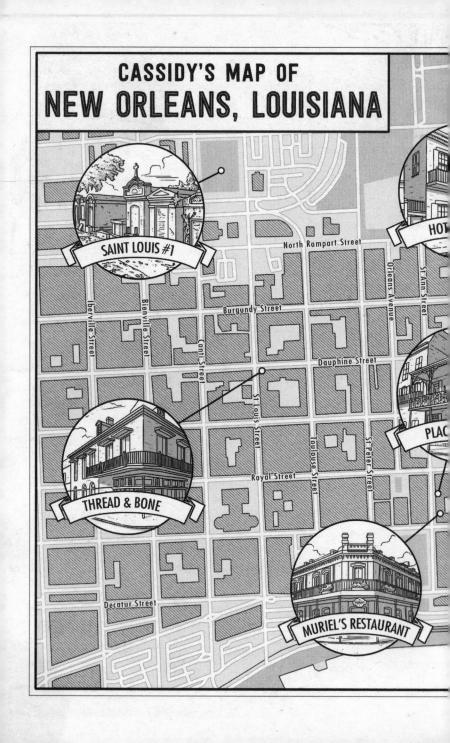

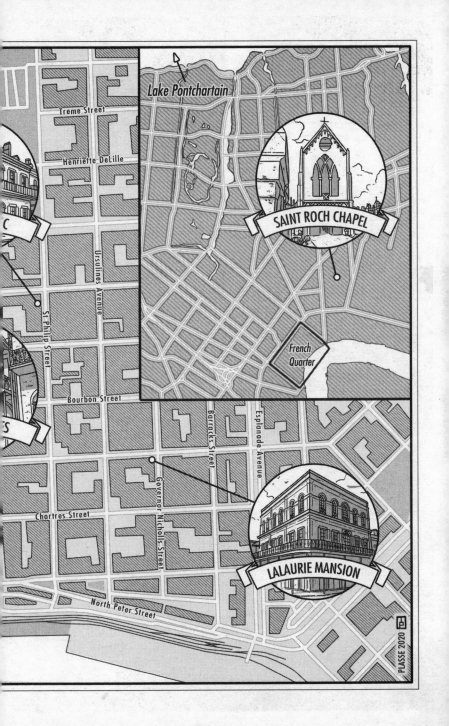

Treme Street

Henriette DeLille

Ursulines Avenue

St Philip Street

Bourbon Street

Chartres Street

Lake Pontchartain

French Quarter

SAINT ROCH CHAPEL

Barracks Street

Esplanade Avenue

Governor Nicholls Street

North Peter Street

LALAURIE MANSION

PLASSE 2020

PART ONE

SUGAR AND SKULLS

CHAPTER ONE

I can think of so many nice ways to wake up.

There's the smell of pancakes in summer, or the first cool breeze of fall. The lazy comfort of a snow day, the world buried beneath blankets. When waking feels easy and peaceful, a slow transition from dreaming to daylight.

And then there's *this*:

The jolt of curtains thrown open onto glaring sun, and the sudden weight of a very large cat landing on my chest.

I groan and drag my eyes open, and see Grim staring down at me, one black paw hovering over my face.

"Off," I mutter, rolling until the cat flops sideways onto the sheets. He shoots me a sour look, lets out a soft cat sigh, and sinks deeper into the bed.

"Rise and shine!" says Mom in a voice that's way too chipper, considering we just got in last night and my body has no idea what time it is. There's a dull thud in my head, and I don't know if it's jet lag or ghosts.

I pull the sheets back up, shivering at the false cold of the hotel's air-conditioning, which has been humming all night. Mom opens the window, but instead of a breeze, a wall of warmth pushes in.

The air is sticky with summer heat.

Down on the street, someone is singing off-key, and the low sound of a trombone wanders up to meet it. A voice howls with laughter. Someone drops something and it rings like an empty pot.

Even at ten a.m., New Orleans is full of noise.

I sit up, my hair a nest of tangled curls, and look around, groggy with sleep. Huh.

When we got in last night, I didn't do much more than wash my face and fall into bed. But now that I'm awake, I realize our hotel room isn't exactly normal. Not that anywhere we've stayed on our travels has been "normal," but the Hotel Kardec is particularly odd.

My bed is nestled in one corner, raised on a little platform. There's a sitting area between my perch and the massive four-poster bed my parents have claimed on the other side of the room. That's not the strange part. No, the strange part is that the whole room is decorated in rich purples and dark blues with gold accents, and silk and velvet are draped over everything, like the inside of a fortune-teller's tent. The drawer handles and wall hooks are shaped like hands: fingers clasped or palms up, reaching.

We left our suitcases in a pile on the polished wood floor, clothes spilling out in our eagerness to change and crash post-flight. And there in the center of the chaos, between my mom's toiletry case and my camera bag, sits Jacob Ellis Hale, best friend and resident ghost.

Jacob's been haunting me since last summer, when I fell in a river and he saved my life. Together, we've faced spirits in Scotland, poltergeists in Paris, graveyards and Catacombs, and more.

He sits cross-legged, elbows resting on his knees, a comic open on the floor in front of him. As I watch, the pages *turn.*

It could be a breeze, but my mom has already closed the window.

And the pages only turn one way, at roughly the pace of a boy reading a book.

We both know he shouldn't be able to do that.

A week ago he couldn't, and now—

"Come on, Cass," says Mom. "Chop-chop."

We're not filming until tonight, so I'm about to protest, when Dad adds, "We're meeting our guide at Café du Monde."

I perk up, curious. Every place we travel for my parents' show, we get a new guide. Someone who really knows the city—and its secrets. I wonder what our guide here will be like. If they'll be a skeptic, or a believer.

Across the room, my parents bustle around, getting ready. Mom wipes a streak of shaving cream from Dad's jaw. He helps Mom with the clasp of her bracelet.

Right now, they're still my parents: clumsy, and nerdy, and sweet. But tonight, when the cameras go on, they'll become something more: the Inspecters, world-traveling, ghost-hunting paranormal investigators, larger than life.

"Your life is pretty large," says Jacob without looking up. "Or at least, pretty strange. I've never really understood how a life changes *size* . . ."

Jacob Ellis Hale, best friend, resident ghost, and constant eavesdropper.

He holds up his hands. "It's not my fault you think so loud."

4

As far as I can tell, his ability to read my mind has something to do with the fact that he pulled me back from the land of the dead, and I pulled him into the land of the living, and we got kind of stuck together. Like hair and chewing gum.

Jacob frowns. "Am I the *gum*?"

I roll my eyes. The thing is, I should be able to read his mind, too.

"Maybe my thoughts are just quiet," he says.

Maybe your head is just empty, I think, sticking out my tongue.

He scowls.

I snort.

My parents turn and look at me.

"Sorry." I shrug. "Just Jacob."

Mom smiles, but Dad raises a brow. Mom's the believer, though I'm not really sure she believes in Jacob-the-ghost or Jacob-the-imaginary-friend-and-convenient-excuse-for-why-her-daughter-gets-into-so-much-trouble. Dad is definitely *not* a believer, and he thinks I'm getting too old for imaginary friends. I agree. But Jacob is hardly imaginary, just invisible, and it's not my fault my parents can't see him.

Yet.

I think the word as quietly as possible, but Jacob still hears. He doesn't seem to catch the dread in it, though, because he stands up and smiles.

"You know," he says, exhaling against the window, "maybe I could . . ."

He brings his index finger to the fog and frowns, concentrating, as he draws a *J*. To my surprise—and horror—the letter shows up on the glass.

I lunge out of bed and wipe it away before my parents can see.

"Killjoy," he mutters, but the last thing I need is Mom and Dad realizing Jacob *is* real, or that I almost died, or that I've been spending every second of free time hunting down ghosts. Somehow, I don't think they'd approve.

Sit, stay, I order as I slip into the bathroom to get dressed.

I pull my hair up into a messy bun and try not to think about the fact that my best friend is absolutely, undeniably, getting stronger.

I free my necklace from under my shirt collar and study the dangling mirror pendant. A mirror, to show the truth. A mirror, to remind the spirits that they're dead. A mirror, to hold them still, so I can break the thread, and send them on.

My reflection stares back at me, uncertain, and I try not to think about the Veil, or the reason ghosts are meant to stay on the other side. I try not to think about what happens to spirits who become real enough to touch our world. I try not to think about my friend Lara Chowdhury, who told me it was *my* job to send Jacob on before he becomes too dangerous, before, before.

I try not to think about the dreams I've had, where Jacob's eyes go red, and the world breaks apart around him, and he doesn't remember who I am, doesn't remember who *he* is, and I have to choose between saving my best friend and saving everything else.

I try not to think about any of it.

Instead, I finish getting dressed, and when I come back out, Jacob is sprawled on the floor in front of Grim, engaged in what looks like a staring contest. I remind myself that Jacob is Jacob. He's not an ordinary ghost. He's my best friend.

Jacob breaks his gaze, glancing toward me, and I know he can hear my thoughts so instead I focus on Grim.

The cat's black tail flicks lazily from side to side, and I wonder, not for the first time, if cats—even totally useless bread-loaf cats—can see more than meets the eye, if they can sense the Veil, and the ghosts beyond, the way I can.

I grab my camera from the floor, loop the purple strap over my head, and load a fresh roll of film. My parents have asked me to document their show behind the scenes. As if I don't have enough on my plate, keeping malicious ghosts from creating chaos.

But hey, everybody needs a hobby.

"I recommend video games," says Jacob.

I peer at him through the viewfinder, sliding the camera's focus in and out. But even when the room blurs, Jacob doesn't. He's always crisp and clear.

This camera, like everything else in my life, is a little strange. I had it with me when I almost drowned, and ever since, it has a way of seeing *more*.

Like me.

My parents, Jacob, and I head down the hall, which is decorated like our room: rich blues and purples, and wall sconces shaped like hands. Most of them are holding up lights. But here and there, a few of the hands are empty.

"Ghost five," says Jacob, smacking one of the open palms. It rocks a little, threatening to fall, and I shoot him a withering look. He flashes me a sheepish smile.

To get downstairs, we bypass the ominous wrought-iron elevator that's only large enough for one and opt for the sweeping wooden staircase instead.

The lobby ceiling's been painted to show a table and empty chairs, as if I'm overhead, looking down—a dizzying effect.

I feel like I'm being watched, and turn to see a man in an alcove, peering out from around a curtain. Only as I get closer, I realize it's not a man but a bust: a copper sculpture of a head and chest. He has a goatee and sideburns, and he's staring intently at me.

The sign on the marble base tells me this is Mr. Allan Kardec.

Jacob leans against it.

"Looks grumpy," he says, but I disagree. Mr. Kardec is frowning, but it's the kind of frown Dad wears sometimes when he's thinking really hard. Mom calls it his clockwork face, because she says she can see the cogs turning behind his eyes.

But there's also something eerie in the statue's gaze. The eyes aren't made of copper, I realize, but glass: dark marbles threaded with wisps of gray.

Mom calls for me, and I turn to see her and Dad waiting by the hotel's exit. Jacob and I back away from the statue's ghostly stare.

"Ready?" asks Dad, pushing open the door.

And with that, we step out into the sun.

The heat hits me like a ball of lead.

In upstate New York, where we usually live, the summer sun gets hot, but the shade stays cool. Here, the sun is liquid heat, even in the shade, and the air is like soup. I swing my arm through it, and feel moisture clinging to my skin.

But the heat isn't the only thing I notice.

A horse-drawn carriage rumbles past us. A hearse goes the other way.

And I'm not even in the Veil. This is the living, breathing version of New Orleans.

We're staying in the French Quarter, where the streets have names like Bourbon and Royal, where the blocks are short and squat, and wrought-iron balconies run like ivy along the front of every building. It's a collision of color, and style, and sound. Cobblestones and concrete, twisting trees and Spanish moss. I have never been somewhere so full of contradictions.

Edinburgh, the first city we went to for the show, was damp and gray, a city of old stones and hidden paths, its history right on the surface. Paris was bright and clean, gold filigree and wide avenues, its secrets buried underground.

New Orleans is—something else.

It's not the kind of place you can capture in a photo.

It's loud, and crowded, and full of things that don't fit, the clop of horse hooves at odds with the honk of a sedan and a saxophone. There are plenty of restaurants, and tattoo shops, and clothing stores, but in between are windows filled with candles and stones, and pictures of saints, and neon signs with upturned palms, and crystal balls. I can't tell how much of it is a show put on for tourists, and how much of it is real.

And on top of it all—or rather, *behind* it all—there's the Veil, full of ghosts, wanting to be heard and seen.

Spirits sometimes get stuck there, caught in a kind of loop of their last moments, and it's my job to send them on.

"Debatable," says Jacob, who would rather pretend that it's totally normal for a girl to hear the *knock-knock-knock* of ghosts and feel the constant pressure of the other side trying to pull her through. "I'm just saying, when has sending ghosts on made your life *easier*?"

I get his point, but it's not about doing what's easy.

It's about doing what's right.

Even if, now and then, I wish I could mute the other side.

A carriage goes by, decked out in red feather plumes and gold tassels, and I follow behind it, trying to get a good photo.

"Hey, Cass, watch out," says Jacob, right before I run straight into someone.

I stagger back, blinking away the darkness. I'm already halfway through saying "Sorry" when I look up and see a skeleton in a pitch-black suit.

And just like that, the world slams to a stop.

All the air rushes out of my lungs, and New Orleans drops away, and I'm back on the train platform in Paris, the day we left, staring at the stranger on the other side of the tracks, wondering why no one else has noticed the smooth white skull beneath the wide-brimmed hat. I'm trapped in my skin, unable to breathe, unable to think, unable to do anything but stare into those empty eyes as the stranger reaches up and pulls away the mask, and there's nothing but darkness beneath.

And I'm falling, through those empty eyes, and back into New Orleans, as the skeleton here steps straight toward me, reaching out a bony hand.

And this time, I scream.

CHAPTER TWO

The skeleton pulls back.

"Hey, hey," he says, recoiling. "Sorry, kid." He lifts his hands in surrender, and they aren't bone at all but flesh, fingertips jutting up from cut-off gloves. "I didn't mean to scare you."

His voice is easy, human, and when he pulls off his mask, there's a face beneath, warm and friendly and real.

"Cassidy!" says Mom, taking my elbow. "What's going on?"

I shake my head. I hear myself mumbling that it's fine, that it was my fault, that he didn't scare me, but my heart is pounding in my chest, so loud it fills my ears, and I have to force myself to breathe as the man walks away. And if anyone thinks it's strange to see a man dressed like a skeleton in the middle of the morning, they don't say. Nobody so much as looks twice as he wanders, whistling, down the street.

"Cass," says Jacob softly.

I look down, and see my hands are shaking. I wrap them around the camera case, squeezing tight until they stop.

"You okay, kiddo?" asks Dad, and both of my parents are now looking at me like I've sprouted whiskers or wings, transformed from their daughter into something skittish, and fragile, and strange.

I don't blame them.

I'm *Cassidy Blake.*

I've never been squeamish. Not when a girl at school got a bloody nose and looked like she'd spilled a bucket of red paint down her front.

Not when I reached into a ghost's chest for the first time and pulled out the rotten remnants of its life.

Not when I climbed into an open grave, or fell through a pile of crumbling bones five stories underground.

But the skeleton in the black suit was different. The memory alone is enough to make me shiver. Back in Paris, when the stranger in the skull mask looked at me from across the platform, it was like they looked straight through me. Like I was a nice warm room, until they threw the windows open, and then everything went cold. In that moment, I had never felt so sick, so scared, so alone.

"Like a Demental," says Jacob.

I blink, dragging my attention back. "What?" I ask.

"You know, the creepy wraithlike monsters in Harry Potter who suck out your life, eat all your joy, and leave you cold."

Oh. He means Demen*tor*.

Jacob has never actually *read* the books, so his knowledge is made up entirely of movie snippets and my constant references—but for once, he's almost right.

It *was* kind of like that. Like I looked darkness in the eye, and it ate up all the light inside me. But Dementors aren't real, and whatever that *thing* was, back in Paris, it was. At least, I think it was.

Nobody else saw it.

Not even Jacob.

But it *felt* real enough to me.

"I believe you," he says, knocking his shoulder against mine. "But maybe you should talk to Lara."

Which may be the *last* thing I ever thought I'd hear Jacob say.

"I know, I know," he says, shoving his hands in his pockets.

Jacob and Lara don't exactly get along. You could say it's a difference of temperament—Jacob's all Gryffindor, and Lara's undeniably Ravenclaw—but it's more complicated than that. Lara's an in-betweener, like me, and her job—which is my job, too—is to send ghosts on to the other side, and Jacob is firmly, undeniably here.

He clears his throat.

Which is exactly where he's supposed to be, I think pointedly.

"Look," he says, "Lara doesn't know everything, but she *does* know a lot of stuff, and maybe she's seen one of these weird skeleton men before."

I swallow hard. Whatever I saw in Paris, it wasn't a man. It was *shaped* like one, more or less, with that black suit and that broad-brimmed hat. But a man has flesh and blood. A man has a face behind his mask. A man has *eyes*.

What I saw?

It wasn't human at all.

As my parents walk on ahead of me, I take out my phone. It's the middle of the afternoon in Scotland, assuming Lara's still staying with her aunt. I send a text.

Hey, can you chat?

Within seconds, she texts back.

Lara:
What did Jacob do now?

"Rude!" he mutters.

I look down at the screen, trying to figure out how to ask about what I saw on the platform.

I bite my lip, searching for the words.

"I think the ones you're looking for are *scary*, and *nicely dressed*, and *soul-sucking skeleton dude*," offers Jacob, but I shoo him away.

Me:
There are other paranormal things, right?
Besides ghosts?

Lara:
You'll have to be more specific.

I start a few texts, deleting them each time. I don't know what's stopping me. Or maybe I do.

I can't always run to Lara. I shouldn't have to. I'm an in-betweener, too. I should know what to do. And if I don't, I should be able to figure things out on my own.

"Sure," says Jacob, "but *you* don't have a dead uncle who spent his whole life researching the paranormal and now haunts the leather chair in your living room."

"No," I say slowly, "but I have you."

Jacob smiles, a little uncertain. "Well, yeah, obviously." He scuffs his shoe. "But I didn't see the skeleton thing."

And there's more to my hesitation. The truth is, I don't want to think about what I saw, or how it made me feel. I don't want to put it into words, because then it will be real.

> Lara:
> Cassidy?

I look around for something else to ask her about. A spray-painted mouth smiles at me from a brick wall, two fangs jutting from the upper lip. An arrow points down an alley and asks the question, *Thirsty?*

I snap a photo with my phone and hit send.

> Me:
> Real?

Moments later, Lara writes back:

> Lara:
> No, Cassidy, vampires are not real.

I can practically hear her posh English accent. I can

picture her rolling her eyes, too. Lara's remarkably skeptical for a girl who can move between the world of the living and the dead.

My phone buzzes again.

Lara:
Are you in New Orleans? I've always wanted to go. It's home to the oldest branch of the Society of the Black Cat.

It's not the first time Lara's mentioned the secret organization. When we met, she was staying in Edinburgh with her aunt and the ghost of her uncle. When her uncle was alive, he was a member, she said, of the Society, a mysterious group that knows all sorts of things about the paranormal.

Lara:
If I were there, I could petition the Society in person and convince them to let me join.

Lara:
If you find their headquarters, let me know.

I glance around again, half expecting to find a sign for the Society right here on Bourbon Street.

Me:
Where are they?

Lara:
I'm not sure. They don't exactly advertise.

Up ahead, Dad's studying the hours of a museum dedicated to poisons, while Mom reads a sandwich board advertising séances. I walk over to join Mom, and I study the icon of the upturned hand, a crystal ball hovering in the air over the palm. I take a photo of the board and send it to Lara.

Me:
What about this? Real?

I watch the three blinking dots that signal she's typing. And typing. Still typing. I don't know why I expected a simple answer, but when the text comes in, it fills my screen.

Lara:
Psychics are real, but séances generally fall under the category of entertainment. This is because, unlike in-betweeners, psychics stay on this side of the Veil, and pull the curtain back to talk to someone on the other side. But séances claim to bring those spirits across the threshold into the land of the living. If the spirits are strong enough to cross over, they generally get out.

Jacob reads over my shoulder, shaking his head.

"She could have just said no."

He's standing in front of a café window, and he squints at a reflection only the two of us can see. He runs a hand through his hair, but it doesn't move. It's always sticking up, just like his superhero T-shirt is always wrinkled. Nothing about him ever changes, because it can't. It hasn't, since the day he drowned.

I'm glad he told me the truth about what happened to him in the river, I really am.

I just can't stop thinking about it. About the Jacob I never got to meet. The one with two brothers and a family and a *life*. He sighs and shoots me a look, and I realize, I'm thinking too loudly. I start humming a song in my head, and he rolls his eyes.

Mom and Dad start walking again, and Jacob and I follow. I'm just about to turn my attention back to Lara's texts when Jacob passes an open doorway. The shop beyond is filled with candles, and tinctures, and charms, and Jacob erupts into sneezes.

"Stupid—"

Sneeze!

"—spirit—"

Sneeze!

"—wards—"

Sneeze!

At least, I think that's what he said.

It's the same reaction he had back in Paris, when Lara sent over protective charms to keep a poltergeist at bay. Apparently, the charms work on all sorts of spirits, even increasingly corporeal best friends.

I take a photo of the shop—the word VOODOO ghosted on the glass—and send it to Lara.

Me:
Real?

I'm waiting for her answer when something catches my eye.

It's a black cat.

It's sitting on the shaded curb in front of a shop called Thread & Bone, grooming one leg. For a moment, I wonder if Grim somehow got out. But of course it's not Grim—I've never seen Grim so much as lick a paw—and when the cat looks up, its eyes aren't green but lavender. I watch the cat stretch, and yawn, and then trot away down an alley. There are probably a ton of black cats in a city like this, but I think of the Society and wonder if it might

23

be a clue. Mom would call that "a little on the nose," but just to be safe I snap a photo of the cat before it disappears. I'm about to send it to Lara when she texts me back about the voodoo shop.

Lara:
Very real.

The text is followed by an XO, and for a second I think she's trying to send me hugs and kisses, which would be very out of character. Then she explains that it's a skull and crossbones—like a bottle of poison. Do not touch.

The mention of a skull reminds me of the skeleton in the suit. Maybe I should just tell Lara about what happened. But before I can, she texts that she has to catch a flight, and then she's gone.

I blow out a breath and tell myself it's okay. I don't need her help. Just because I saw the skull-faced stranger once doesn't mean I'll see it again. Once is a glitch, an accident. No reason to be worried.

"Yeah," says Jacob, sounding skeptical. "I'm sure it will all turn out fine."

CHAPTER THREE

At Café du Monde, the air tastes like sugar.

The café sits at the edge of Jackson Square: a giant courtyard full of people—tourists, but also performers. A woman stands on an upturned bucket, painted head to toe in silver. She's dressed like a dancer, but she doesn't move until someone drops a coin into her palm. A man plays a saxophone in the shade, and the sound of a trumpet rises from the other side of the square. The two melodies sound like they're talking.

We grab a table beneath the green-and-white-striped awning. Mom and Dad order coffee, and I order iced tea, which comes in a large, sweating plastic cup. The drink is mercifully cold, but sweet enough to make my teeth hurt.

A dozen fans make lazy circles over our heads, churning the air without cooling it, but despite the heat, Dad is clearly in his element.

He looks out at the bustling square.

"New Orleans is a marvel," he says. "It was founded by the French, given to the Spanish, used by pirates and smugglers—"

Jacob and I both perk up at that, but Dad presses on.

"Sold to the United States, scarred by slavery, consumed by fire, ravaged by flood, and rebuilt despite it all, and that's just the shape of it. Did you know the city has forty-two cemeteries, *and* it's home to the longest bridge in the US? The Lake Pontchartrain Causeway—you can't see one side from the other—"

Mom pats his arm. "Save some for the show, darling," she teases, but he's on a roll now.

"This city has more history than hauntings," he says. "For one, it's the birthplace of jazz."

"And home to voodoo and vampires," says Mom.

"And *real* people, too," presses Dad, "like Pere Antoine and Jean Lafitte—"

"And the Axeman of New Orleans," adds Mom brightly.

Jacob shoots me a look. "I really hope axe is a kind of instrument and not—"

"He went around chopping people up," Mom adds.

Jacob sighs. "Of course he did."

26

"Back in 1918, he terrorized the city," says Dad.

"No one felt safe," says Mom.

They're sliding into that TV show rhythm, even though there are no cameras, just me and Jacob, hanging on the edge of their words.

"He was a serial killer," says Mom, "but he loved jazz, so he sent a letter to the cops and said he wouldn't strike any house that had a full band playing in it. So for weeks, music filled the city streets, even more than usual. It spilled out of houses day and night, a cacophony of jazz."

"Did they catch him?" I ask.

And Mom blinks, eyebrows going up as if she got so caught up in the story, she never thought about how it ended.

"No," answers Dad. "They never did."

I look around, wondering if the axeman's ghost is still wandering these streets, a hatchet on one shoulder and his head cocked, listening for a saxophone, a trumpet, some promise of jazz.

Mom breaks into a smile. "Hello! You must be our guide."

I twist around in my seat, and see a young Black man wearing a crisp white button-down shirt, the sleeves rolled to his elbows. Behind wire-framed glasses, his eyes are light brown, flecked with green and gold.

"Professor Dumont," says Dad, rising to his feet.

"Please," he says, in a kind, smooth voice. "Call me Lucas." He shakes Dad's hand, and then Mom's, and then mine, which makes me like him even more. "Welcome to New Orleans."

He sinks into a plastic chair across from us and orders coffee and something called *beignets*.

"You're staying in the Hotel Kardec?" he says as the waiter leaves.

"We are," says Mom.

"It's named for someone, isn't it?" I ask, remembering the statue in the lobby, with its far-off gaze and studied frown. "Who was he?"

Lucas and Dad inflate at the exact same time, both about to speak, but then Dad nods for Lucas to go on. Lucas smiles, and straightens a little in his chair.

"Allan Kardec," he says, "was the father of Spiritism."

I've never heard of Spiritism, and Lucas must be able to tell, because he explains.

"Spiritists believe in the presence of a spirit realm, and the . . . entities that inhabit it."

Jacob and I exchange a glance, and I wonder if Kardec could have known about the Veil. Perhaps he was an in-betweener.

"You see," continues Lucas, "Kardec believed that spirits—phantoms, ghosts, if you like—existed there, in that other place, but that they could be communicated with, summoned by mediums."

"Like in a séance?" I ask.

"Exactly," says Lucas.

And suddenly the decorations back at the hotel make sense. The velvet curtains, the outstretched hands, the painting on the lobby ceiling—the table and chairs, empty and waiting.

"There is a séance room in the hotel," Lucas adds. "I'm sure they'd be happy to give you a show."

Mom and I say "Yes!" at the same time Jacob says no, but since I'm the only one who can hear him, the vote doesn't count.

A plate arrives, piled high with pieces of fried dough

covered in powdered sugar. Not dusted, really, but buried beneath the sugar, white mountains like snow over the mounds of dough.

"What are these?" I ask.

"Beignets," says Lucas.

I pick one up, the fried dough hot beneath my fingers, and bite down.

The beignet melts a little in my mouth, hot dough and sugar, crispier than a doughnut and twice as sweet. I try to say how good it is, but my mouth is too full, and I end up breathing out a tiny cloud of powdered sugar. It is *heaven*.

Jacob eyes the beignet mournfully as I pop the rest in my mouth. He folds his arms and mutters something like *"Not fair."*

Lucas takes one, and somehow manages to eat it without spilling sugar all over himself, which I'm pretty sure is a kind of superpower. Even Dad, who's a bit of a neat freak, has to dust some powder off his sleeve.

Mom, meanwhile, looks like she walked through a snowstorm. Sugar dots her nose and her chin; there's even some on her forehead. I snap a photo, and she winks.

My own shirt is streaked with white, my hands sticky, but it was totally worth it.

"Well, Professor Dumont," says Mom, wiping her hands. "Do you believe in ghosts?"

Our guide steeples his fingers.

"It's hard to live in a place like this and not believe in something, but I prefer to focus on the history."

It's a very diplomatic answer.

"Better than my husband," says Mom. "He doesn't believe in any of it."

Lucas lifts a brow. "Is that so, Professor Blake? Even after all your travels?"

Dad shrugs. "As you said, I prefer to focus on the history. That part, at least, I know is real."

"Ah," says Lucas. "But history is written by the victors. How can we know what really happened if we weren't there? We are, all of us, speculating . . ."

At that point, Dad and Lucas launch into a deep discussion about the "lens of history" (Dad) and the past as a "living document" (Lucas) and I stop paying attention.

The show binder sits on the table, the cover dusted with

streaks of sugar. I pull it toward me, flipping past Scotland and France to the third episode, marked by a single red tab.

> *THE INSPECTERS*
> *EPISODE THREE*
> LOCATION: NEW ORLEANS,
>   LOUISIANA
> "LAND OF LOST SOULS"

"Well, that's promising," says Jacob, reading over my shoulder as I skim the list of filming locations.

> 1) THE PLACE D'ARMES
> 2) MURIEL'S RESTAURANT
> 3) ST. LOUIS NO. 1, NO. 2, NO. 3
> 4) LAFAYETTE CEMETERY
> 5) THE OLD URSULINE CONVENT
> 6) THE LALAURIE MANSION

It all sounds fairly innocent, but I know by now that looks can be deceiving.

When the beignets are gone and the glasses are empty, everyone gets to their feet. Lucas dusts off his hands, even though he doesn't have a speck of sugar on him.

"See you tonight?" asks Dad.

"Indeed," says Lucas. "I think you'll find this is a different city after dark."

That night, Lucas is waiting for us in the hotel lobby, along with our film crew: a guy and a girl, a mismatched pair, linked only by the cameras hanging from their hands. They introduce themselves as Jenna and Adan. Jenna is small and bubbly and white, the ends of her black hair dyed electric blue, and a dozen silver chains draped around her neck. Adan is a giant, a towering guy in a black T-shirt, tattoos wrapping every inch of his olive skin.

He catches me staring at them and flexes so I can see the Christian cross on his bicep, the Egyptian eye on his forearm, the pentacle near his elbow. Some of the symbols I don't recognize—a knot of triangles inside a loop, and a bold black mark that looks like a crow's foot.

"That's an algiz," he says. "It's a rune."

He goes on to explain it's not a crow's foot, but an elk's. I study the other symbols. I've seen people wearing one or two of them, but Adan has at least seven.

"What are they all for?" I ask.

"Protection," he explains. A little thrill runs through me as my own hand drifts to the mirror around my neck.

"From what?"

He shrugs. "Everything."

Jenna leans in and pats his arm. "Adan likes to keep his bases covered." Her voice drops to a fake whisper. "He's not a big fan of things that go bump."

"Keep talking," Adan says. "One day you'll see a ghost, and you'll get it."

Jenna sighs dramatically. "I wish!" she says, pouting. "No one has ever haunted me." Her eyes flick to my mirror pendant. "Cool necklace."

"Thanks," I say, twirling it between my fingers. Jacob winces when the mirror twists his way, and I close my hand over the glass before he can catch sight of his reflection. It happened once, back in Scotland. I can still see him the way he was in the glass: gray, and dripping wet from the river, and undeniably dead.

Jacob clears his throat, and I force a smile.

"Ready?" asks Lucas, his voice steady and sober, as if the answer might be no.

We step out of the Hotel Kardec, and the Veil rises to meet me. Without the sun glare and the heat, the press of ghosts is even stronger, tapping on my skull, swimming at the edges of my sight.

Music spills out of bars and off corners, but I can hear the music *beneath* the music. Ghostly tendrils of jazz drifting on the lukewarm breeze.

Mom squeezes my shoulder.

"Do you hear that?" she says, eyes dancing. "The city is waking up."

I'm pretty sure we're not listening to the same thing, but still, she's right.

And so was Lucas.

New Orleans *is* a different city after dark.

The heat has faded to a drowsy warmth, but there's nothing sleepy about the French Quarter. The streets are buzzing with people, crowds milling on curbs, drinking and singing.

Laughter spills down the street, and cheers pour out of open doors, and jazz instruments duel for space, and under all of it is the Veil. The worlds of the living and the dead feel like they're colliding around me.

We pass a group on a vampire tour—they're all carrying frozen drinks, the cherry-red contents staining their mouths, and wearing white plastic fangs, their cheerful energy at odds with their inspiration.

I'm so distracted by it all, I almost run into Adan, who's stopped on the curb, camera raised. They've started filming.

Mom and Dad are standing in front of a redbrick building that's clearly a hotel. It has a wrought-iron balcony and a white sign that reads PLACE D'ARMES. To the right, there's an archway, just wide enough for a carriage, fronted by an iron gate.

Nothing special, nothing strange. But when I look through that archway, the space beyond cloaked in shadow, the hairs stand up on the back of my neck, and the Veil presses like a hand against my back.

I know if I'm not careful, it will push me through.

"Here in New Orleans," says Dad, addressing the camera, "almost everything you see was built on the ruins of something else. Twice the French Quarter has burned down, once in 1788, and again only six years later. Countless blazes have broken out since, consuming rooms, or buildings, or blocks."

"Perhaps that's why this city is so haunted," muses Mom. "One of the reasons, anyway. Everywhere you step, everywhere you stay, was once home to something—and someone—else."

"Take this hotel, for example," says Dad, gesturing at the building behind them. "The Place d'Armes."

Mom rests her hand on the iron gate. "Long before it was a hotel," she says, "it was a schoolhouse. When fire swept through the Quarter, many of the children were trapped inside." Her eyes meet the camera. "They never got out."

I shiver, despite the summer heat.

The gate creaks open beneath Mom's hand, and together she and Dad turn, and step out of the streetlight and into the dark.

"We'll just wait out here," calls Jacob, but I'm already following my parents through the archway.

Jacob sighs, and trudges after me.

The moment I step through the gate, the Veil greets me.

Smoke tickles my nostrils, and I hear a wave of giggles and the shuffle of small feet.

"Hide," whispers a voice.

"Not there," hisses another.

I reach out to steady myself against the nearest wall, and the Veil reaches for my hand, wraps itself around my wrist. I hear laughter, the high sound of children's voices in the dark.

And then, out of nowhere, another voice. Not like the others, faint and far away. No, this one's closer. It's low and deep, not a child's voice, barely a voice at all, more like a rasp of air, a door groaning open.

"We are coming for you."

I gasp and twist free, pushing off the wall and stumbling backward into Lucas.

He looks down, silently asking if I'm okay.

I nod yes, even though my heart is racing. Even though that voice rattled through me like rocks, sharp and wrong, and left me feeling . . . cold.

Did you hear that? I think at Jacob, who has his arms folded tight across his chest.

"The creepy children?" he asks.

38

I shake my head. *The other voice.*

His forehead crinkles. He shakes his head. And suddenly, I can't wait to get far away from the Place d'Armes, and whatever's lurking beyond that wall. For the first time, I have no desire to step through the Veil and learn more.

"They're still here, those children," says Mom, her voice echoing through the carriageway. "Guests have heard them running in the halls, and some have woken to find their things moved around the room, their coins and clothes stacked like pieces in a game."

"As we'll soon see at our next location," says Dad, "not all the spirits in this city are so playful."

We retreat back down the carriageway, and Lucas pulls the gate shut behind us. It closes with a scrape, a sigh. I should feel relieved, but I don't.

As my parents head down the street, I look back at the archway, squinting into the dark.

I lift my camera, peering through the viewfinder, and slide the focus in and out until I can almost, *almost,* *almost* see someone standing beyond the gate. Small fingers wrapped around the bars. But there's another shape looming behind, a pitch-black shadow, darker than the dark. It twitches forward, a sudden, jerking step, and I drop my camera.

I catch it before it hits the ground. But when I lift the lens to my eye again, the frame is empty.

The shadow's gone.

CHAPTER FOUR

The lights have gone on in Jackson Square.

Old-fashioned yellow lampposts cast long shadows, and a bright beacon illuminates the large white church off to the side, making it look like a tombstone. The square isn't empty, but the energy has changed, the daytime performers thinned to a handful of musicians, each playing a weak and wandering tune.

The Veil is usually a rhythmic beat, but here, tonight, it's like too many instruments playing at once, each one slightly off-time or out of tune.

The Veil reaches for me, but so does Jacob.

I feel his hand close around mine, and look down at our fingers. Mine solid, and his . . . something else, no longer air or even mist. There's a faint glow right where our palms meet, and I swear, I can see the color bleeding into his skin where it touches mine: the light, the *life*, flowing into him.

"Cassidy!" calls Dad.

Jacob drops my hand, and we both turn, searching.

My parents aren't in the square anymore. They're standing on the corner with the rest of the crew, in front of a restaurant, and for a second I think it's time for dinner. But then I see the sign, the restaurant's name in elegant black script.

Muriel's.

I recognize the name from the show binder, and my curiosity is louder than my hunger.

The restaurant looks like half the buildings in the Quarter—two stories tall, with iron rails and massive white-framed windows. But I know there's a reason it's on the Inspecters' list. Something waiting beneath the surface.

Mom told me once to think of it like paint in an old house. It gets covered, layer by layer, and you might not know a blue wall used to be red until you chip away at it.

So that's what my parents do.

They find the red paint.

The only difference is, we have a history of the house. We've been told where to look.

"And the red paint is dead people," says Jacob.

And that, I think.

We step through the doors, and I brace myself for the Veil, but the first thing I feel isn't the patter of ghosts, it's the sudden, merciful wave of air-conditioning. I shiver with pure relief, the muggy night air replaced by an ice-box cool.

I feel my limbs sigh into it.

The restaurant on the ground floor is huge. Green ivy drips from planters hung like chandeliers, and big round tables have been draped in white linens. A dark wooden staircase leads up to a landing.

"Oh, hey," says Jacob, pointing at the walls. They've all been painted red. I roll my eyes.

"It's just a metaphor," I say, but as I stand in the front hall, I have to admit, I'm starting to feel *something* besides the air-conditioning.

It's early for dinner but there's already a decent crowd, the chatter of guests, clinking glasses and cutlery drowning out the *tap-tap-tap* of ghosts, any whispers beyond the Veil. But the other side leans against me, like a tired friend, and when I swallow, it feels like there are ashes on my tongue.

My hand drifts up to the mirror around my neck.

Ever since my accident I've been able to see and hear the

other side. Sometimes, I can feel it, too. But in Muriel's, I can *taste* it.

And it tastes like smoke. Not stale smoke, the kind long soaked into curtains, but fresh, and hot. It burns my eyes and scratches at my throat.

Was there a fire here, too? I wonder. I don't realize I've asked the question out loud until Lucas answers.

"In 1788," he says. "The Good Friday Fire tore through the French Quarter, destroying most of the houses."

"Out of eleven hundred buildings," adds Dad, "eight hundred and fifty-six were burned."

Jacob whistles softly as Lucas nods.

"This house, like most of the ones in the Quarter, was rebuilt."

"This city is a phoenix," says Mom. "Always rising from the ashes."

Fire and ash.

No wonder I can taste smoke.

A hostess from the restaurant appears to greet us. She seems breathless, and has that *I'm on my way can't stay and chat* energy. "You must be the Investigators," she says, scanning our motley group.

44

"Inspecters," corrects Mom.

"I was told you have what you need, yes, I see you do, very well, we're short on staff today, so I'm afraid I can't spare a guide—"

"No worries," says Dad, gesturing at Lucas. "We brought our own."

"Great," she says, "all right, welcome to Muriel's . . ." And with that, she's already gone.

"Well," says Jenna, her camera on her shoulder. "Which way to the ghosts?"

Jacob and I look at each other. Mom and Dad scan the restaurant. Adan shifts his weight from foot to foot.

But Lucas nods at the dark wooden stairs. "Up."

As we climb the stairs, the noise from the restaurant fades.

Mom pulls out her EMF meter—a device used to measure spectral energy—and switches it on. The box hums with a low static.

When we reach the space at the top of the stairs, the EMF meter begins to whine. Other people would take it as a warning, but to Mom it's just an invitation. It gets louder as she walks, but I'm pretty sure it's because Jacob is trailing behind her.

The room upstairs is a kind of lounge: deep plush sofas and chairs piled with cushions. It is mercifully dark and cool. Mom heads for a pair of not-quite-open doors, red light spilling through the gap. She stops, the EMF meter rising into high static.

"What have we here?" she asks in a singsong voice.

"Ah," says Lucas. "That would be the séance room."

Mom lets out a delighted *mmmm*. She nudges the doors open, looks back at us with a face full of mischief, and slips inside.

Dad chuckles and follows, Lucas on his heels.

Jenna plunges in next as if it's a pool.

Adan hangs back a moment, lets out a low breath, as if psyching himself up, then goes in.

Jacob and I are still standing in the lounge area.

"That," he says, pointing, "looks like a very comfy couch."

I roll my eyes. We're not here to nap.

"But we could be," he complains as I head for the doors.

I don't have to look back to know he's there, though, following me through.

The séance room is bathed in red. It's like walking into a darkroom, that deep crimson light, *just* bright enough to see by. I expected a table and chairs, like the painting on our hotel ceiling, but this room is as cluttered as an antique store. Pillows are piled on old sofas and ornate chairs. An Egyptian sarcophagus leans against one wall. There's a sculpture of a woman dancing, a floor lamp casting her shadow against a patterned wall. There are faces everywhere: A trio of Venetian masks smile and grimace. An old man stares out from a dusty portrait. Two old-fashioned women in elegant dresses glance up from a painting in an ornate frame. Tinny music whispers through a speaker somewhere out of sight, an eerie, old-sounding song.

A giant mirror sits on the floor, so old it's gone silver. Jacob catches sight of it and jerks his gaze away, but I stop to stare at myself, my curls gone wild with humidity, the camera hanging around my neck. The weathered surface makes me look like an old-fashioned photo. I step closer, turning the pendant on my necklace out, so the mirrors catch each other, reflecting again and again as far as I can see. An infinite tunnel of Cassidys.

As I stare into the endless reflection, the ordinary world goes quiet in my ears. The sound of my parents talking to the camera, the tinny music, and the far-off noises of the restaurant all seem to fade as the Veil *leans* into me.

It's like when you know someone's watching you. When you can *feel* the weight of their gaze. And I know if I ignore it for too long, the nudge will become a hand gripping my wrist, and it will drag me through, into the world of ghosts.

But I can't go through, not yet.

I turn, putting my back to the mirror, and tuck the pendant under my collar.

Mom and Dad are sitting on the other side of the room, on a fancy sofa. Lucas catches my eye and holds one finger to his lips. The red light on Jenna's camera tells me they're rolling.

Dad runs his hand down the arm of the sofa. "Welcome to the séance room of Muriel's."

"Now this," adds Mom, "is a place that's home to more than history."

Dad rises to his feet. "It is not a kind past," he says

soberly, buttoning his tweed jacket. "Like in much of New Orleans, the shadow of slavery touches everything. Some insist that the building first raised on this plot of land was used to house slaves before they were auctioned off. The building was torn down, and in its place, a grand house was built, only to burn down in the great blaze of 1788, along with most of the Quarter."

Mom produces a single green coin—a poker chip—and turns it idly between her fingers.

"A man named Pierre Jourdan bought the property and erected the mansion of his dreams, only to lose the estate in a poker game," she says. "Devastated, Jourdan took his own life up here. Some say in this very room."

For a moment, no one speaks.

I hear the smallest breath hiss between Adan's teeth. The only other sound is that tinny old-fashioned music and the whisper rising to meet it, the murmur of voices from the other side.

"Jourdan is believed to haunt the rooms of his old house," Mom goes on. "Moving plates in the downstairs restaurant, shuffling glasses in the bar, and, sometimes, simply lounging in one of these chairs." Mom bounces to her feet. "But of course, he's not the only ghost that calls Muriel's home."

My parents head for the doors, the film crew following close behind.

I hang back, and Lucas glances over his shoulder, a silent question in his eyes. I pretend to be fascinated by one of the masks, pretend I didn't even notice everyone was leaving.

"I'll catch up," I say, waving him on.

"Yeah," says Jacob, "why would we want to head back into the nice, busy, living restaurant when we could stay here with the horror movie music and the wall of faces?"

Lucas lingers a moment, too, as if trying to decide what to do, but in the end, he nods and goes. It feels like the handshake back at Café du Monde. Like he sees me as somebody, instead of just somebody's kid.

And then Jacob and I are alone in the séance room, with the smell of smoke, and the whispers in the walls, and the red light staining everything.

"Cass," whines Jacob, because he knows what I'm thinking.

Fire and ash, and the drum of ghosts.

Spirits, trapped and waiting to be sent on.

I reach out, and feel the invisible curtain brush against my fingers. The boundary between the land of the living and the world of the dead.

All I have to do is close my hand around it, pull the gray film aside, and step through.

I know what to do—but again, I hesitate, afraid of what else might be waiting beyond the Veil.

There's always a risk, of course.

You never know what you'll find.

An angry spirit. A violent ghost. One that wants to steal your life. Or cause chaos.

Or there could be something else.

A skull-faced stranger in a trim black suit.

"You know," says Jacob, "fear is a perfectly rational response, the body's way of telling you *not* to do something."

But if I waited until I wasn't scared, I'd never go through.

Fear is like the Veil. It's always there. It's up to you to still go through.

My hand travels to the cord at my collar and I tug the necklace out, let the mirror pendant rest faceup in my palm.

Look and listen, you say when you see a ghost. *See and know.*

This is what you are.

Well, this is what I am.

This is what I do.

This is the reason I'm here.

I catch hold of the curtain and pull it aside, stepping through into the dark.

CHAPTER FIVE

For one terrible second, I'm falling.

A downward plunge, a single shocking gasp of cold, the air knocked from my lungs—

And then I'm back on my feet.

The Veil takes shape around me, in mottled shades of gray. I take shape, too, a ghostly version of myself, washed out save for the bright blue-white ribbon glowing in my chest. My life. Torn, and stitched back together. Stolen, and reclaimed.

I press a hand to my chest, muffling the light as I look around the séance room. It ripples and shifts in my vision. The red light is gone, the room lit only by the soft glow of lamps. The masks leer down from the walls. The faces stare out from the paintings.

"Oh, look, it's just as creepy," says Jacob, appearing beside me. Here in the Veil, he's solid, real, another reminder that I'm out of place.

53

He didn't have to come.

But he always does.

"Rule number four of friendship," he says. "Stick together. Now, can you just find a ghost and send them on so we can go back?"

As if on cue, a door slams down the hall.

I pull the necklace over my head and take a few steps toward the sound, but the moment I move, my vision doubles, blurs. The room multiplies, sliding in and out of focus around me. Furniture shifting, appearing, disappearing, changing, burning, smoke and laughter, light and shadow, all of it so disorienting I have to squeeze my eyes shut.

I don't understand.

I've crossed into the Veil countless times. Back home, and in Scotland, and in France. I've seen places where the Veil is empty, nothing but a stretch of white, like unmarked paper. But this is different. This is more than one Veil in the same place.

I remember what Dad said about Muriel's, how it had been torn down and rebuilt, how it had belonged to several families and lived several lives.

And suddenly this muddled, overlapping scene makes sense.

Because the Veil isn't really *one* place. It's a collection of remembered spaces, stitched together, each tethered to a ghost, their life, their death, their memories. That's why some parts are empty—no ghost to hold them up.

And that's why this one is full.

Because Muriel's doesn't belong to just one ghost.

It belongs to several. Each with their own story. And I'm standing in all of them.

"It's giving me a headache," says Jacob, closing one eye and then the other.

He looks silly, but it gives me an idea. I let go of the mirror pendant and lift my camera instead, peering through the viewfinder. I slide the lens in and out until only one version of the house comes into focus at a time.

In one, I'm in the plush séance room, all elegant tapestries and low rosy light.

In another, I'm standing on rough wooden boards, the clink and slide of chains somewhere below.

In a third, the room is hot and dark, smoke seeping up between the floorboards.

I don't know where to start.

And then another door slams. Loud and close. I slide the focus just in time to see a man surge across the doorway and down the hall. He's not in the building on fire, or in the slave quarters. He's in the ornate house.

"No, no, no," he mutters, dragging his hand along the banister. "It's gone."

I catch up as he rounds the corner, follow him into a room with a poker table, chips piled in tiny mountains before empty chairs.

"It's *gone*."

In a violent motion, he sweeps his arm across the table, scattering the chips. They fall like rain around him. I step closer, and he rounds on me.

"They took it all from me," he snarls, and I know this must be Mr. Jourdan, the gambler who lost his whole house, and then his life.

In another version of the house, someone wails, the sound sudden and sharp. It catches me off guard, and in that second, Mr. Jourdan lunges forward and grabs my shoulders.

"Everything is *gone*," he moans.

And I forget I'm gripping the camera instead of the mirror until I hold it up toward his face and nothing happens. The ghost looks at me, and then down at the lens, and then past it, at the curl of light inside my chest.

And something in him *changes*. His eyes darken. His teeth grit.

A second ago, he was a desperate man, trapped in his last moments. But now he's a hungry ghost. A spirit, longing for what it's lost.

I reach for the mirror pendant as he reaches for my life, and he might have gotten there first if a bucket of poker chips hadn't hit him in the side of the head. Jacob has excellent aim.

It gives me just the time I need to get the mirror up between us.

The ghost goes still.

"Look and listen," I say as his eyes go wide.

"See and know," I say as his edges ripple and thin.

"This is what you are."

It's like an incantation. A spell. Say the words, and the ghost goes clear as glass. I reach through his chest and take hold of the brittle thread inside. It once was a life, as bright as mine. Now it comes away in my hand, dark and gray, already crumbling to dust.

And just like that, Mr. Jourdan fades and disappears, and so does his version of Muriel's.

My vision blurs, and it's getting a little hard to breathe. For a second I think it's just my body, warning me I'm not supposed to stay too long in the Veil. And then I remember the smoke.

"Uh, Cass," says Jacob.

And I see the smoke rising from the ground floor, seeping through the walls.

The wail comes again, and I realize it's not someone but some*thing*, a siren, a horn, a warning to get out.

I reach for the curtain, but it doesn't rise to meet my fingers.

I try again, grasping for the gray cloth between worlds, but the Veil holds tight.

"No time," shouts Jacob, pulling me toward the landing.

We race down the stairs, even though down is hotter, down is the direction of fire curling through the house. It stings my eyes and burns my throat, and the Veil shifts and slides around us. One step, the house is on fire and people are shouting. The next, it's dark. And I don't know which Veil I'm in with each passing step, but I know I don't want to be here when the building comes down.

We reach the foyer, the front door hanging open on its hinges.

Outside, I see the Quarter is burning.

And it's not.

It's a mess of overlapping scenes, buildings on fire and unburnt, alarms ringing one second and music filling the air the next. Veils tangled together with the same chaotic energy of jazz. I squeeze my eyes shut as something cracks over our heads.

I look up in time to see a burning beam crashing toward us, and then Jacob's pushing me forward, through the door and the curtain and the Veil, seconds before the beam collapses into smoldering wood and fiery ash.

The world shudders into life and color, and I'm sitting on the hot pavement in front of the bustling restaurant, listening to the clank of silverware and laughter. The scent of smoke fades a little with every breath.

"Could have stayed in the lounge," says Jacob, sagging back on the sidewalk. "Just relaxed like normal people."

"We're not normal," I mutter, brushing off the Veil like cobwebs.

"There you are," says Mom, appearing in the doorway. "Hungry?"

I'm not thrilled about going back into Muriel's, but the food looks really good.

Jenna and Adan stash their camera equipment under the table, and Lucas puts away his notes as dishes arrive. Mom and Dad have this rule that when we travel, I can order whatever *I* want, but I have to take one bite of whatever *they* get. Which is how I end up with a plate of fried chicken and biscuits, but find myself facing down Mom's bowl of gumbo, and Dad's shrimp and grits.

Gumbo, it turns out, is a kind of stew poured over rice. It's rich, and full of flavors—and pieces of things I don't necessarily recognize—but it tastes good. *Grits*, on the other hand, look like grainy porridge, like something that was supposed to dissolve but didn't.

But a deal is a deal, so I brace myself and take a bite of the grits, and they're . . . good. Salty and buttery and simple, creamy without being rich. It reminds me of grilled cheese sandwiches, and chicken nuggets, the food I crave when I'm sick, or sad, or tired.

Comfort food.

I take another spoonful, and Dad offers to trade plates, but I think I'll stick with my fried chicken. I glance around, trying to keep track of Jacob. I see him wandering from table to table, eavesdropping on other people's conversations. Poking saltshakers and nudging napkins, having staring contests with people who can't see him. He wanders into the kitchen and comes back a few minutes later, looking pale.

"You don't want to know how they make lobster," he says.

I roll my eyes.

When we're all stuffed and the plates have been cleared away, Adan leans his elbows on the table and says, "I've got a ghost story for you."

Everyone perks up.

"It's about the LaLaurie," he adds, and the mood at the table changes around me.

"What's that?" I ask. I remember the name from the list of locations in the binder.

"The LaLaurie Mansion," explains Lucas, his voice quiet and tense, "is considered the most haunted place in New Orleans."

"And for good reason," adds Mom, and for once, the topic of ghosts doesn't seem to make her cheerful. There's a crease in her forehead, and her mouth is a pale pink line.

"What happened?" I ask, looking around, but no one seems willing to tell me.

Adan clears his throat and presses on.

"Right," he says, "the LaLaurie Mansion has a gruesome past, but *this* story isn't about way back then. This one's new. It happened just a few years ago. People keep buying the house, you know, but no one stays too long. Well, a big-shot actor, he buys the house, and asks a friend of a friend of mine to stay in it, to watch the property. Alone."

Jacob and I exchange a look, and I don't need to read my friend's mind to hear him thinking, *Nope.*

"So she goes to bed that night, and she's just falling asleep when her cell phone rings. She doesn't answer, just rejects the call. But an hour later, it rings again. This time, she's annoyed, so she silences the phone, tries to go back to sleep. An hour later, it rings *again*, and she finally looks to see who's calling her in the middle of the night."

Adan lets the question hang over the table. And then he smiles, just a little, the way Mom does when she hits the best part of a story.

"It was the landline in the house," he says. "Where she's the only one home."

The table erupts into noise.

Jenna says, "OH MY GOD," and Mom applauds, and Dad laughs and shakes his head, and chills run across my skin, the kind I love, no danger, no fear, just the thrill that happens when you hear a good story.

"Well, on that note," says Mom as we stand to leave, "who's up for a séance?"

CHAPTER SIX

"I f you'll follow me . . ."

The voice belongs to Alistair Blanc, the Hotel Kardec's resident Spiritist.

"The proper title is Master of Spirits," he said when he met us in the lobby tonight. Apparently Lucas called to schedule a séance for us earlier today, after Mom and I offered our enthusiastic yes at Café du Monde.

The Master of Spirits is a small white man, with short silver hair and a sharp goatee, deep-set eyes, and a long thin nose topped by a pair of little round glasses. And he's currently leading us through a door near Kardec's copper bust and into a narrow hall, so dark we practically have to feel our way to the end. He picks up the edge of a velvet curtain, and holds it aside.

"Come in, come in. Don't be shy," says Mr. Blanc, ushering us through into a dimly lit space. "Your eyes will adjust to the dark."

This séance room is nothing like the one at Muriel's. There's no clutter, no tinny music, just a stuffy quiet. There's velvet everywhere, the space draped like a tent, so it's impossible to tell what size it really is. But it feels too small for six people and a ghost.

Lucas came along with us, and Jenna, too, but she left her camera supplies in the lobby with Adan, who seemed a little too eager to stay behind and watch their stuff. ("He's not a huge fan of small spaces," she whispered as we walked away, and I couldn't help but think, *Good thing he wasn't with us down in the Catacombs beneath Paris.*)

A chandelier hangs in the center of the room, an elaborate sculpture of hands, each holding a candle in a foggy glass jar. Six high-backed chairs sit like thrones around a table covered in black silk. A large black rock, like a giant paperweight, sits in the center. The rock seems more ornamental than functional, but I can't stop looking at it. And the longer I look, the more my eyes play tricks on me.

If you've ever stared into a campfire, or the woods, or a blanket of snow, you understand. Your brain gets bored and starts doodling. Showing you things that aren't there.

I stare at the stone until I can almost see shapes. Smudged faces in the dark.

Chairs scrape back, and I blink, dragging my attention back to the room, shivering.

It should be warm in here, stifling even, with all the velvet, but the air is cold, a draft sliding over my arms and ankles as I sit down.

I lift my camera, slide the focus in and out, but all I see is the room as it is.

No hint of the Veil.

No glimmer of something more.

I take a photo of the narrow space, even though the only way I'd be able to capture the full room is from overhead. That makes me think of a ghost story Mom once told me, of hotel guests and the photos they found on their camera, the ones they couldn't possibly have taken, because of the angle, which was right over their bed.

Mr. Blanc takes his seat in a throne at the table. Candles rise at his back, and a large bell hangs on a hook by his elbow.

He gave us permission to film the séance—seemed eager, even, to be on camera—but Lucas said that wouldn't be necessary. I get the feeling Lucas shares Dad's opinion when it comes to this kind of thing.

According to Dad, séances are a *spectacle* of the supernatural.

"Most people don't believe in a thing unless they see it for themselves," Dad had explained on our way back to the hotel. "And if they see it, they'll believe it, even if it isn't real."

"Who knows what's real?" Mom had said, swinging an arm around my shoulder. "But *anything* is possible."

"Please join hands," instructs Mr. Blanc once we're all seated.

Well, all of us except Jacob, who's busy circling the room, walking the narrow path between the backs of the chairs and the velvet-curtained walls. He looks behind one of them and confirms there are air grates back there, causing the cold draft, the gently swaying velvet.

"How does a séance work?" asks Mom, with an enthusiasm reserved for the strange and the morbid.

Mr. Blanc strokes his goatee. "That depends. To reach out to someone specific, someone you've lost, I need a possession, something of theirs to call them forth. Or, if you like, I can simply reach out to the spirit realm and see who answers." He considers us. "I am only a humble conduit, but I believe that, for some such as you, the spirits would have *much* to say."

"I certainly do," says Jacob, who's stroking his chin in a near-perfect imitation of Mr. Blanc.

Don't do anything, I think pointedly.

Jacob sighs. "You're no fun." He gestures at the room. "This place is like a spectral playground!" he says, right before his arm passes through one of the candles. The flame shudders and goes out.

Mr. Blanc raises a brow. "The spirits, it seems, are eager to begin."

I scowl at Jacob, who flashes me a bashful grin. *Sorry*, he mouths.

"Do you wish to call on a specific spirit," asks Mr. Blanc, "or shall I open the gates and see what comes through?"

I tense a little, but remind myself of what Lara said. Séances aren't real. And unless Mr. Blanc is an in-betweener, which I seriously doubt, there's no risk of him letting anything through.

"Ohh," says Mom. "Let's let the ghosts decide."

"Very well." The lights dim around us, and Dad, ever the skeptic, raises a brow. Mom kicks him lightly under the table. Jenna squirms excitedly in her seat. Lucas looks straight ahead, his face carefully blank.

Mr. Blanc clears his throat, and I realize I'm the only one who hasn't joined hands.

"Don't worry," says Mr. Blanc. "The spirits cannot hurt you."

Well, that's a straight-up lie, I think, remembering all the ghosts I've met in the Veil who've tried to kill me.

But this is just a game. A bit of fun, as Lara would say.

So I take the hands on either side of me, completing the circle.

I can still feel the Veil, but it's no stronger here than it was out in the street. If anything, it's softer, the tap of ghosts reduced to a gentle press. I stare at my own warped reflection in the black stone centerpiece.

"Close your eyes," says Mr. Blanc. "And quiet your minds. We must create a clear channel."

If Lara were here, she would scoff, and say that isn't how it works. That we're on one side and they're on the other, and unless someone died really close to this spot, there's probably no one to talk to.

But Lara's not here, so everyone, including the Spiritist, closes their eyes.

Everyone except for me.

Which is why I see the strings, the seams, the tricks that make it easy to believe.

I see the pale smoke spilling between a break in the velvet curtains. I see Mr. Blanc shift something between his teeth. I see his shoe move under the table, just before we hear a knock.

Everyone opens their eyes, blinking in surprise at the fog, the subtle changes in the room.

"Is anyone there?" asks Mr. Blanc.

Jacob holds his breath, and I don't know if it's because he's resisting the urge to cause a scene, or if he genuinely thinks he might be summoned and forced to answer.

But when Mr. Blanc speaks again, his voice is higher, stranger, a little muffled, as if there's something in his mouth, which I know there is.

"My name is Marietta," he says. "Marietta Greene."

It's like watching a ventriloquist, except Mr. Blanc is both the master and the doll. His lips are always moving.

"I don't know where I am," he continues in that strange, squeaky voice. "It is so dark, I think they must have boarded the windows and locked the doors . . ."

It sounds like a speech; the words trip out too easily.

I feel the cold draft, and slight tremor of the table, all the things I know are tricks, part of the performance. But I don't feel anything ghostly.

And then I do.

The air in the room changes. The draft drops away, and the mist holds still, and the bell at Mr. Blanc's elbow begins to ring, even though he never touched it.

Mr. Blanc stares down at the bell, and for a second, he looks totally surprised.

But then his head lolls forward, like a puppet without any strings. His hands drop from Jenna's and Mom's, landing on the table with the dull smack of dead weight.

For a moment, he's as still as a statue, as still as a *corpse*, and Jacob slips behind my chair, as if he plans to use me as a shield.

Nice, I think, right before Mr. Blanc's mouth hinges opens and a voice spills out. A voice that isn't really a voice at all, but wind against old windows, a draft beneath a door. A rasping whisper, a rumble in the dark. The same voice I heard at the Place d'Armes.

And this time, it's speaking to *me*.

PART TWO

THE VOICE IN THE DARK

CHAPTER SEVEN

We have seen you, little thief.*

The words slip between Mr. Blanc's teeth, hissing like steam from a kettle.

"Light burning in your chest."

The words roll over me like a chill, carrying that hollow fear, that strange emptiness. The same cold terror I felt on the platform in Paris.

"Once you stole from us. And once you fled."

The words keep spilling out of Mr. Blanc's mouth, but they don't belong to him. There is no projection now, no drama, no flair. If anything, his delivery is eerily flat, his voice empty of emotion.

"But now you cannot hide."

As the Spiritist speaks, something moves inside the black stone centerpiece. I watch as it rises to the surface. At first, it's nothing but a pale white streak. But soon, I can see its hinged jaw and its empty black eyes, and I know it's a skull.

And I can't look away.

"*We have seen you.*"

I can't move.

"*And we will find you.*"

I'm back on the train platform as the skeleton in the black suit reaches up to pull away its face.

In the séance room, Mr. Blanc's head drifts up, his eyes open and empty. Like something else has climbed inside, like something else is looking out.

"*We are coming for you, little thief.*"

The Spiritist leans forward, unseeing, and my hand goes to the mirror at my throat. An anchor in the storm.

"*We will find you, and balance the scales.*"

Mr. Blanc's fingers dig into the silk tablecloth as the voice that is not a voice gets stronger in his throat.

"*We will find you and return you to the dark.*"

I drag in a shuddering breath. The skull in the black stone and the Spiritist at the table both swivel suddenly toward me, those empty eyes narrowing, and for a moment I'm certain that the thing inside Mr. Blanc can see me, and I jerk backward as—

CLANG!

Jacob shoves both hands into the bell at Mr. Blanc's side.

It tips and falls, ringing through the narrow room and tearing the Spiritist from his trance. He sits, bolt upright, looking as shocked as I feel. He blinks rapidly, and clears his throat. The fog has faded. The draft is back. The black stone is empty. The presence is gone. And for a long moment, no one speaks.

And then Jenna claps her hands. "That was *awesome!*" she squeals.

But I can't breathe.

The fear that was pinning me down is gone, the weight lifted, and I violently shove myself up to my feet, knocking my chair against the wall.

"Cassidy?" asks Mom, but I'm already rushing toward the velvet curtain.

I can't get out of there fast enough.

I push aside the velvet curtain—or I try, but I pick the wrong one, and find only a wall beyond.

Panic works its way through me, and I can hear Jacob telling me to calm down, can hear Dad asking if I'm all right. But my heart is a wall of noise in my ears, and I just have to get *out*.

I finally find the right curtain and shove it aside, stumbling back down the hall and into the lobby.

We have seen you.

I pull the necklace from beneath my collar, gripping the mirror tight.

And we will find you.

I run across the lobby, past Adan, who's lounging with his legs up on the equipment, and out through the doors into the night.

The air is warm, and the street is full. Not just with a crush of tourists, but with a river of strangers in brightly colored masks, a parade of people playing music and painted up like a sea of skeletons.

They're everywhere. I can't get away. So I race back into the hotel. My shoes squeak on the lobby's marble floor as Mom and Dad appear, Jacob and the film crew just behind.

"Bit over the top," Dad's saying.

But Mom pulls me into a hug. I try to laugh it off, apologize for getting overwhelmed, as if it was just a scary séance. As if I'm just a girl afraid of ghosts.

We will find you and return you to the dark.

Lucas polishes his glasses and says, "I think that's enough for tonight."

He doesn't look at me when he says it, but the words still feel like they're directed at me. I want to say no, say I'm fine, but my head's too full of fear and questions. I'm relieved when Mom yawns and Dad agrees, saying tomorrow is a fresh start.

We say good night and go upstairs.

The hall to our room suddenly feels menacing, the light unsteady. The bronze hands reaching out from the walls all seem to be reaching for *me*.

Back in our room, Mom and Dad make small talk about the day, and I retreat to my bed and busy my hands with my camera. Jacob sits down beside me.

"Was that . . . " he asks, trailing off.

I let out a small, unsteady breath, and nod. I think so.

"What *is* that thing, Cass?"

"I don't know!" I hiss. I shake my head, and think it again, softer. *I don't know. I don't know. I don't—*

"Okay," Jacob says. "But we both know someone who will."

I reach for my cell, before remembering the time. It's the middle of the night in Scotland. Lara's asleep.

"I'm pretty sure this is one of those 'in case of emergency, break glass' situations," says Jacob. "Call her. Wake her up."

I shake my head and send her a text instead. I don't write, *I think there's some kind of grim reaper stalking me.* I don't write, *Apparently I stole something and it's coming to take it.* I don't say, *I'm scared.* Though all of those things are true. But they don't feel like the kind of thing you send over text, so instead, I just write:

Me:
SOS

I toss the phone aside and get off the bed, and I'm halfway to the bathroom when the cell rings with an incoming video call. I scoop it up, relief flooding me at the sight of Lara's name on the screen.

I hit answer, and Lara Chowdhury appears, her black hair braided into a crown around her head.

"Did you know," she says in that prim, proper way, "that some people think SOS stands for Save Our Ship, or Save Our Souls, but really it's something called a bacronym.

80

The abbreviation came first, and the phrase came next. Anyway, what's wrong?"

But I'm still distracted by the fact she's up. "Shouldn't you be asleep?"

"It's only nine forty-five."

I look at the clock on the bedside table. "But it's nine forty-five here, too."

"Yes," she says dryly, "that *is* how time zones work."

"Is that Lara?" calls Mom, brushing her teeth. "Hi, Lara!"

"Lara says hi," I call back, before carrying the phone out into the hall, careful to shut the door behind me—the last thing I need is Grim getting loose.

"Where are you?" I ask softly, peering at the screen.

"I'm in Chicago," answers Lara, gesturing to the pale marble steps behind her, as if that's an indicator. "I did tell you I was getting on a plane. Mum and Dad gave a lecture tonight at a museum, and they invited me to come." She lets out a soft, almost-inaudible sigh. Lara's parents are archaeologists, but I've never seen them. It sounds like Lara doesn't see much of them, either. "We were supposed to stay on for a few more days, see the sights together, but

I guess they got an opportunity they couldn't pass up. One that doesn't involve their daughter. They're leaving first thing tomorrow for Peru. And I guess I'll be going back to Scotland."

"By yourself?"

Lara bristles. "I'm more than capable of navigating an airplane, Cassidy."

She swallows, looks away for a second. Lara's the kind of girl who holds all her feelings right against her chest, like a book she doesn't want to share. But I can hear the sadness in her voice.

"I'm sorry," I say, and I'm afraid it's the wrong thing, because I hear a hitch in her breath.

"It doesn't matter." She clears her throat. "A stamp in the passport, right?" she adds, sounding like she's trying to convince herself more than me. "Now. How's New Orleans? Have you found any clues about the Society?"

I'm about to tell her about the black cat I saw when Jacob cuts in. "Something is hunting Cassidy."

I shoot him a look. I was about to tell her.

Lara blinks. "You mean a ghost? Like the Raven in

Red?" she asks, referring to the hungry spirit that tried to steal my life in Scotland.

I shake my head. "Not . . . exactly."

She gives me a look that says *explain* and so I do, the best I can.

Jacob leans against the wall as I pace, and I tell Lara about what I saw back in Paris: the man who wasn't a man, the skull mask that wasn't a face, and the eyeless dark beyond. I tell her how I fainted, how it felt like I was being emptied out. I tell her about the voice I heard in the archway, and then the one that interrupted the séance: what it said to me, about stealing, and fleeing, and being found, and returned to the dark. I tell her everything, and Lara listens, her face going first slack, and then tight, but she doesn't say anything. Her expression isn't chiding or stern. If anything, Lara Chowdhury looks *scared*. I've never seen her scared before.

"When did it happen, in Paris?" she asks softly. "When did you see it for the first time?"

Jet lag makes everything stretch, so it takes me a second to do the math.

"Two days ago."

"Why didn't you tell me?" she snaps.

Jacob shoots me an *I told you so* look, and I can't believe that he and Lara finally agree on something.

"I didn't think it was a big deal," I say, which isn't entirely true, but isn't exactly a lie. "I didn't want it to be a big deal. I wanted it to be a bad dream. The kind of thing you shake off and leave behind. And, if it *was* something, I thought I could handle it myself."

Lara studies me, her anger glaring through the screen.

"Cassidy Blake," she says slowly, "that is the stupidest thing I have ever heard. Being an in-betweener does *not* mean you have to face things on your own. It means you have to ask the *right* people for help. People like *me*."

I swallow hard, and nod. I'm afraid to ask, but I have to know.

"Lara," I say. "What *is* it? The creature in the black suit?"

She sucks in a breath, and holds it. When she finally exhales, the air sounds shaky in her throat.

"That creature," she says, "is an Emissary. A messenger."

"A messenger of what?" I ask.

"Death."

CHAPTER EIGHT

The word hangs there, taking up all the space.

"Wait," says Jacob, pushing off the wall, "like, lowercase death, or uppercase Death?"

"Does it matter?" I hiss.

"Both," says Lara. "Emissaries come from the place *beyond* the Veil. They're sent out into the world to hunt for people who've crossed the line, and come back."

"People like us," I say.

People who've almost died.

For me, it was the river. I don't know what happened to Lara, but I know it must have been bad, must have been close, one-foot-in-the-grave kind of close. That's how you become an in-betweener.

She nods. "My uncle told me about them once. He said they're like fishermen, casting out their lines. Watching for movement in the water. Waiting for something to snag on a hook."

"Have *you* ever been hunted by an Emissary?" I ask, sinking onto one of the benches lining the hallway.

Lara purses her lips and shakes her head. "No. I've always been very careful. I go into the Veil, I send a spirit on, I get out. I don't go for a swim, so to speak. I don't make a splash."

Lara doesn't need to say that *I* do just that. I've always let my curiosity get the best of me; I can't help exploring. It's what attracted the Raven in Red to me in Scotland. It's how the poltergeist found me in Paris. And now . . .

"Some people just make waves," Lara goes on. "It doesn't matter why, or how. What matters is, you snagged the line. But it hasn't reeled you in just yet."

"Is this the part where you tell us not to worry?" asks Jacob.

Lara shakes her head. "No, this is the part where I tell you to *hide*."

I shudder as the Emissary's words come back to me.

You cannot hide.

"How am I supposed to do that?" I ask.

"You need to stay with your parents, and the film crew.

Don't wander off. And if you can help it, *don't* cross the Veil."

I think of how I felt in Muriel's. Of how hard it is to resist the pull of the other side.

"Because it'll be able find me there?"

"It can find you *anywhere*. It can clearly move through the world of the living and the land of the dead. But you'll stand out more beyond the Veil."

"And if it catches me . . ."

But I already know.

It will take me back into the dark.

"No matter what happens," Lara says, "just stick together." Her eyes narrow on Jacob. "I mean it, ghost. Don't let it find her alone."

Lara's attention shifts back to me. "Cassidy," she says, and I've never heard her say my name like that, full of warning, and friendship, and fear.

I swallow hard. "How do I beat it?"

Lara is quiet for a long moment. And then she says, "I don't know."

Her voice is small, and I realize she's just as scared as I

am. Then she shakes her head, clears her throat, and says, "But I'll find out."

And just like that, the Lara I know is back. And I'm grateful to have her.

"Be careful," she says, and ends the call.

I look down at the darkened screen for a moment, then slump back, letting my head thunk against the wall. I look up and see a bronze hand hovering over me. I fold forward, my head in my hands as Jacob sits down next to me.

"You know," he says slowly. "When the Raven in Red stole your life and trapped you in the Veil, I was scared. I know you couldn't tell, because I'm so good at acting brave—"

I snort.

"But I was terrified. I didn't know how we were going to get out of it. But we did. You did."

I press my palms into my eyes.

"And then when that creepy poltergeist kid starting causing all that trouble in Paris, and we had to go down there in the Catacombs, I was so scared. Not that you could tell."

"What's your point?" I ask softly.

"It's okay if you're scared this time, Cass. Because I'm not. I'm not scared because I know we're going to get through this."

I lean my shoulder against his, and for the first time, I'm grateful he's more than a ghost, grateful for the slight pressure of his arm against mine.

"Thanks, Jacob."

The door to our room swings open, and Dad pops his head out into the hall. "There you are." Grim pokes his head out, too, gets one paw over the threshold before Dad ducks to catch him. "No you don't," he says, scooping the cat under his arm. "Bedtime, Cass."

I get up, and follow. I climb into bed, one hand tight around my mirror charm, while Jacob sits on the floor next to Grim.

Jacob usually wanders off at night—I've never known where, but ghosts don't exactly need sleep—but tonight, he stays close. A ghostly sentinel. Having him there makes me feel safe.

Or at least, saf*er*.

"Rule number ninety-six," he says. "Friends don't let friends get snatched away by creepy skeletons."

I groan, and pull the blankets up over my head.

Outside, people are still laughing and singing in the streets. New Orleans is one of those places that never sleep.

And apparently, neither will I.

At some point I finally drift off, and when I do, I dream.

I dream of the séance room in the Hotel Kardec. I'm sitting in one of the chairs, and there's no one else there, and I can't turn around, but I can feel the curtain move behind me, can feel something reaching for me.

"We will find you," it whispers, bone fingers curling around the chair.

I shoot to my feet, and suddenly I'm on the Metro platform in Paris.

The train pulls away, and I see the stranger in the dark suit, tipping its hat. The skull mask beneath that seems to grimace and smile and grimace again, and then it lifts a gloved hand to the mask and pulls it away, and there's nothing underneath, nothing but darkness and gravity.

I fall forward again, out of Paris.

I twist in time to see the bridge, my bike wrapped around

the rail, before I hit the water's surface and crash down into the river.

An icy shock, and then I'm under. I'm sinking. Drowning.

It is so cold and dark beneath the water.

A world of black—and blue.

A blue too bright to be natural light.

I look down, and see the ribbon glowing in my chest, the blue-white thread of my life, only visible in the Veil. It shines, bright as a beacon in the dark, but there's nothing else to see. I'm all alone in the river.

Or so I think.

A hand grabs my wrist, and I gasp, twisting around.

But it's just Jacob, his blond hair floating around his face.

"It's okay," he says, and his voice is crystal clear, even though we're underwater. "It's okay," he says again, wrapping his arms around me. "I'm here."

But instead of pulling me up toward the surface, he pulls me down, down, away from the light, and the air, and the world overhead.

I try to say his name, say *wait*, but all that comes out are bubbles. There is no air. I can't breathe. I try to tear free, but his grip is iron, is stone, and when I twist enough to see his face, there is no face at all. Just a skull mask, the eyes empty and black. A skeletal smile, set in bone.

And when he speaks again, the voice is deep, and low, and unlike anything I've ever heard. I feel it in my bones.

"You belong here," it says, holding me tight until my lungs scream, and the light inside my chest flickers, and dims, and goes out.

And we sink down through the bottomless dark.

I sit up with a gasp.

Morning light glares through the window, and through Jacob, who's perched on the windowsill, tugging at a loose thread on his shirt. Mom and Dad bustle around, getting dressed.

I collapse back into the sheets, pulling a pillow over my head.

I feel headachy and wrong, and I can still taste the river in my throat, can hear the voice like a vibration in my chest.

You belong here.

Grim pads across the bed and paws at the pillow.

"Up and at 'em, sleepyhead," says Mom. "Places to visit, spirits to see."

"You know," says Jacob, "I wonder if she'd be so fond of ghosts if she could see them."

I groan and roll out of bed.

Mom is even more cheerful than usual, and I don't find out why until we're at breakfast in the hotel restaurant.

"Cemetery day!" she announces, the way a normal person might say, "We're going to Disneyland!"

I look from Mom to Dad, a biscuit halfway to my mouth, waiting for one of them to explain.

Dad clears his throat. "As I mentioned, there are forty-two cemeteries in the city of New Orleans."

"That seems excessive," says Jacob.

"Please tell me we're not going to all forty-two of them," I say.

"Goodness, no," Dad answers, "that would be impractical."

"It would be a fun challenge," says Mom, her face falling a little, "but no, we simply don't have the time."

"We are, however, going to six of them," says Dad, as

if six is a perfectly ordinary number of cemeteries. He ticks them off on his fingers. "There's St. Louis Number One, St. Louis Number Two, St. Louis Number Three . . ."

"Somebody really dropped the ball on naming," mutters Jacob.

"Lafayette, and Metairie—" continues Dad.

"And St. Roch!" adds Mom, sounding giddy.

"What's so special about St. Roch?" I ask, but she only squeezes my arm and says, "Oh, you'll see."

Jacob and I exchange a look. Mom's excitement is *always* a sign of trouble. And truth be told, I'm not in the mood for any surprises.

But Lara warned us to stay together, and cemeteries are usually pretty safe, as far as spirits go.

It can't be worse than the séance.

CHAPTER NINE

We meet up with Lucas and the film crew in Jackson Square. The air is sticky again today, but the sun has been blotted out by clouds, the low, dark kind that warn of storms.

"Is it always this hot?" I ask Jenna and Adan while Mom and Dad chat with Lucas about the day's schedule.

"Only in June," says Jenna. "And July. And August."

"And May," says Adan.

Jenna nods. "And September," she adds. "And sometimes April and October. But March is pretty nice!"

I try to laugh, but I feel like I'm melting.

I look around. The square is beginning to feel almost familiar, with its clashing music, its buskers and tourists. Despite the brewing weather, people linger all around, selling jewelry—pendants and charms designed to ward off evil or bring good luck.

"Hey, you."

The voice comes from a young white woman in a lawn chair, perched beneath a blue-and-pink umbrella. At first I assume she's talking to someone else, but she looks right at me, and hooks her finger.

"Come here," she says.

I've heard my fair share of fairy tales; I know you're not supposed to go with strangers—especially when you're being hunted by a supernatural force. But she's just sitting there, in the open. And as far as I can tell, she's perfectly human.

I glance over at my parents, deep in conversation with the crew, and then I drift toward her, Jacob on my heels.

The woman's hair is cut in a violet bob and she has freckled skin. There's a fold-up table at her knees, with a large deck of cards facedown on top.

"Name's Sandra," she says. "Want to have your fortune told?"

I consider the question, and the person asking it.

Sandra doesn't look like a fortune-teller.

In my mind, fortune-tellers are old, draped in velvet and lace, their skin weathered and their eyes deep. They don't have purple hair and chipped nail polish. They don't sit in lawn chairs under blue-and-pink umbrellas. They don't wear flip-flops. But if I've learned anything this summer, it's that things aren't always as they seem.

"The first one's free," she says, fanning out a deck of cards. They're beautiful, the backs decorated with swirling lines, suns and stars and moons. They were silver once—I can tell by the shine—but they've been worn away to gray.

Sandra turns the cards over, and I realize there are no hearts, no spades, no diamonds or clubs. Instead there are swords and cups, wands and rings. And scattered in among those, strange paintings of towers, and jesters, and queens.

They're *tarot* cards.

I see a heart driven through with knives. Three wands crossed like a star. A single glowing ring. I shiver at the sight of a skeleton astride a white horse.

Sandra doesn't put on an act. She doesn't change her voice, lace it with mystery or theater. She just turns the deck facedown again, fans the cards between her fingers, and says, "Choose."

I look down at the deck and ask, "How?"

The backs of the cards are all the same. Nothing but suns and stars and moons. No way to tell what I'm picking.

"The cards will tell you," she says, and I don't really understand, until I do. My hand drifts over the deck, the paper edges worn soft, like silk, under my fingers. And then my hand stops. There's a pull, right under my palm, a steady draw, like the Veil rising to meet my fingers.

I draw the card from the deck, holding my breath.

When I see the picture, I exhale. There's no grim reaper, no hangman's noose, nothing particularly ominous. The card is upside down, but when I turn it around, I see a girl, blindfolded, holding a pair of swords, their blades crossed in front of her.

She looks *strong*, I think, but when I glance up, the fortune-teller is frowning.

"The Two of Swords," she murmurs.

"What does it mean?" I ask.

Sandra tucks a strand of purple hair behind one ear and assembles her face into a mask of calm, but not before I catch the worry darting across her features. She takes the card, pursing her lips as she studies the image.

"Tarot can be read two ways," she says, "upright and reversed. The meaning changes depending on which way the card is drawn. But the Two of Swords is a difficult one, no matter how you draw it."

She runs her chipped pink fingernail along one sword, stopping where it hits the other.

"Upright, this card signifies a crossroads. You will have to choose one road, but when you do, the other will be lost. There is no victory without defeat, so you do not want to choose at all, but you must. And no matter what you choose, you will lose something. Or someone."

Jacob tenses beside me, and I try so hard not to think of him, of his growing power, of Lara warning me again and again to send him on. But maybe it isn't about Jacob at all. Maybe it's about the Emissary, about me.

"But your card was upside down," Jacob whispers, "so that means the opposite, right?"

I voice his question, but the fortune-teller only shakes her head.

"Not exactly," she says. "*This* card doesn't have an opposite. It's like the crossed swords themselves. No matter how you look at them, they form an X. Reversed, the Two of Swords still signals the same challenge, the same choice. It means, no matter what you choose, you cannot win without losing, too. There are no right answers."

"Well, that's stupid," mutters Jacob. "You can't just change the rules based on the card. She *said* there were two readings—"

I shake my head, trying to think.

"Can I draw again?" I ask.

"No sense doing that," Sandra says with a shrug. "It's your card. You picked it for a reason."

"But I didn't know what I was picking!" I say, panic worming through me.

"And yet, you chose."

"But what am I supposed to do? How do I know which road to choose if neither one is right?"

The fortune-teller eyes me steadily. "You'll make the choice you need to make, not the one you want." Her mouth tugs into a crooked smile. "As for your future, I'll tell you everything I can," she says, adding, "for twenty bucks."

I dig my hands in my pockets and find a couple of coins, but one is a pound from Scotland, and the other a euro from Paris. I'm about to ask my parents if I can borrow some cash when Dad appears like a shadow at my shoulder.

"What have we here?" He looks down at the cards. "Ah, tarot," he says, his face unreadable. "Come on, Cass," he says, tugging me gently away from Sandra and the Two of Swords.

"I need to know," I say, and he must be able to tell how shaken up I am because he stops and turns back, not toward the fortune-teller, but toward me. Dad kneels, looking up into my face.

"Cassidy," he says in his steady scholar's tone, and I expect him to explain that fortune-telling isn't real, it's just a trick, a game. But he doesn't say that. "Tarot isn't a crystal ball," he says. "It's a mirror."

I don't understand.

"Tarot cards don't tell you what you don't already know. They make you think about what you *do*."

He taps the spot, just over my heart, where my mirror pendant sits beneath my shirt.

Look and listen. See and know. This is what you are.

Words I've only ever said to ghosts.

But I guess they do apply to living people, too.

"Those cards just make you think about what you want, and what you're scared of. They make you face those things. But nothing can predict your future, Cassidy, because futures aren't predictable. They're full of mysteries, and chances, and the only person who decides what happens in them is you." He kisses my forehead as the rest of the group comes over.

"Oh, tarot cards!" says Mom, beelining for the fortune-teller.

"The first one's free," says Sandra, fanning out the weathered deck, but Dad catches Mom's hand.

"Come along, dear," he says. "Those graveyards won't visit themselves."

Jacob and I fall in step behind them.

I hold the card in my mind.

The girl, blindfolded. The two swords crossed before her chest.

You cannot win without losing, too.

And I know what I'm afraid of.

That I don't know how this ends.

CHAPTER TEN

I don't mind cemeteries.

They're usually pretty peaceful, at least for me. See, ghosts in the Veil are tied to the place they *died*, and most people don't die *in* graveyards. They just end up there. Every now and then you get a wandering spirit, but on the whole, they're quiet spaces.

"So are libraries," says Jacob, scuffing his shoe on the sidewalk.

I roll my eyes as we pass through the gates of St. Louis No. 1. To my surprise, there's no grass—just gravel and stone, interrupted by weeds. Pale crypts crowd the space, some polished and others grimy with age. Some even have wrought-iron gates.

"New Orleans is known for many things," says Mom, and I can tell by her voice that the cameras are rolling. "But it's especially famous for its cemeteries."

"And the people buried within them," says Dad, stopping

before a stark white tomb. Small stone planters, filled with silk flowers and slips of paper, are on either side of the sealed door. The stone walls of the tomb are scratched with Xs. On the ground in front of it, people have left a strange pile of offerings: a tube of lipstick, a bottle of nail polish, a vial of perfume, a silk ribbon, and a chain of plastic beads.

"Here lies Marie Laveau," Dad says, "considered by many to be the Voodoo Queen of New Orleans."

Voodoo. I think of the shops we passed yesterday, with their brightly colored pouches and dolls, the word stitched into curtains and stenciled on glass. And I remember Lara's skull-and-crossbones warning. *Do not touch.*

"Born a free woman," Dad goes on, "Laveau opened a beauty salon for the New Orleans elite, and gained a following as an accomplished voodoo practitioner . . ."

I look at Lucas, the two of us hanging back from the group.

"What *is* voodoo?" I ask him softly.

"Not to be trifled with," he answers. But I keep staring at him until he realizes I want a real answer. He tugs off his glasses and begins to clean them for the third time in half an hour. I'm beginning to see that it's a habit, something to do while he thinks, the way Mom chews on pens and Dad rocks back and forth on his heels.

"Voodoo is a lot of things," Lucas says slowly, weighing his words. "It's a set of beliefs, a form of worship, a kind of magic."

"Magic?" I say, thinking of wizards and spells.

"Perhaps *power* is a better word," he says, setting the glasses back on the bridge of his nose. "The kind of power that's tied to a people, and a place. New Orleans voodoo is steeped in history, in pain, just like this city."

"Laveau's power is believed to linger here," Mom's saying now. "Long after her death, people have come to ask for help, marking their request with an X." She gestures to one of the chalk crosses. "If Laveau grants the wish, people return to circle the mark."

Sure enough, a few of the Xs have faint rings around them. I wonder if I should ask Marie Laveau to protect me from the Emissary. I look down at the gravel, searching for a bit of white rock so I can make an X, but Lucas stops me.

"Don't be mistaken, Cassidy," he says. "It isn't as simple as granting wishes. You've seen the shops in the Quarter, selling charms for luck, and love, and wealth, right?"

I nod.

"Most are for tourists. Voodoo isn't just about lighting a candle, or buying a trinket. It's a trade. A matter of give and take. Nothing gained without something sacrificed."

The tarot card glows in my mind.

Give and take.

No way to win without losing.

The crew has moved on to another grave. Lucas starts toward them, and I follow, before realizing Jacob's not with me. I look back at Marie Laveau's tomb, and see him, crouching to examine the offerings left at its base, and I wonder what I'll have to give up in order to win.

Halfway through St. Louis No. 2, it starts to rain.

A lazy drizzle, little more than mist. I huddle beneath a stone angel, its wings just wide enough to keep me dry, but Jacob doesn't have to worry about getting wet. He stands on top of a nearby crypt, head tipped back as if enjoying the storm.

The rain falls through him, but I swear, it bends a little around his edges, tracing the lines of his floppy blond hair, his narrow shoulders, his outstretched hands.

I lift my camera and snap a photo, wondering if I'll catch the outline of a boy, arms spread in the rain.

Jacob notices the camera, and grins, and then he slips, almost loses his footing.

He catches himself, but a shingle comes loose beneath his shoe. It skitters down the roof and crashes to the ground, interrupting one of Mom's stories.

They all turn toward the sound.

Jacob grimaces. "Sorry!" he calls to people who can't hear him, and I just shake my head.

I don't think about the fact that *ghosts* shouldn't be able to bend rain or knock shingles off roofs. I don't think about what happens if he keeps getting stronger. I don't think about what it means for Jacob, for us. I don't think about anything but *not* thinking about it.

And the not thinking is loud enough for Jacob to look at me, and wince.

I'm grateful when it's time to move on.

We take a cab to St. Louis No. 3 (I wanted to take a horse-drawn carriage, but apparently they don't go beyond the French Quarter) and from there to Metairie Cemetery, a sprawling graveyard that used to be a racetrack.

If I listen, I can hear the thundering hooves, the rush of air against my back. It takes all my strength not to cross the Veil, just to see the spectral racers on the other side. But it's easier to resist after Dad says the track was used as a Confederate campsite during the Civil War.

No wonder this place isn't as quiet.

But as we walk down the cemetery's wide avenues, lined with pale stone crypts, something drags at me. I turn, searching for the source, but all I see are graves. And yet, now that I've noticed, I can't shake it. It's like a compass needle, drawing my attention north. North, past the walls of the graveyard. North, toward something I can't see.

But I *feel* it, leaning against my senses, not a pull but a push, a warning deep inside my bones.

And I'm not the only one who feels it.

Jacob stares in the same direction, a rare frown creasing his face.

"What is that?" he asks, shivering slightly.

I catch up to Lucas.

"Hey," I say, keeping my voice down since Mom and Dad are filming. "What's that way?" I ask, pointing in the direction of the tug. Lucas pulls up a map on his phone.

I squint down at the grid of streets, looking for another graveyard, or a monument, something to explain the eerie draw, but there's nothing. Just neighborhoods. Block after block of ordinary houses running all the way out to Lake Pontchartrain. The vast expanse of water intersected only by the long, thin bridge.

I remember Dad talking about that bridge. He said it wasn't haunted, but then, there must be plenty of ghost stories my parents *don't* know, ones they haven't heard. But we're too far from the lake and the bridge for it to be the *tap-tap-tap* of ghosts.

Lucas puts his phone away, but my attention keeps going back toward the strange pull. I lift the camera to my eye, sliding the focus back and forth, as if it will show me the source of the pull, but all I see are blurry headstones. I'm still peering through the viewfinder when Mom calls, "That's a wrap!" and it's time to go.

We grab lunch in the Garden District, a place where all the houses are draped in Spanish moss and look like smaller versions of the White House, columned and proud. And then it's on to Lafayette, which is apparently only Lafayette

No. 1 (they really aren't that good at coming up with names for graveyards here, but I guess when you have forty-two of them, it's easy to run out of options).

The rain has trailed off, but the clouds still hang low, as if it might start again at any second. The world is gray, and full of shadows.

"For such a vibrant city," says Mom, "people love to spend time with the dead."

And I can tell that she's about to start a story.

The cameras trail her down a row of tombs, and we follow.

"A few years ago, a couple was staying at a hotel here in the Garden District when they decided to take an afternoon walk to explore this cemetery."

"As you do," says Jacob.

As if she can hear him, Mom smiles. "It might sound like an odd way to spend the day, but people come from far and wide just to tour the graveyards. They treat them like art galleries, museums, history exhibits. Some come to study, or pay respect to the dead, but others simply like to wander among the quiet crypts."

Her steps slow as she talks.

"On their way, the couple met a young woman, traveling

alone, and she asked them if they knew how to get to Lafayette.

"'You can come with us,' they said. 'We are going there ourselves.'

"And so the three set out together, the couple and the young woman, who said her name was Annabelle. They walked, and chatted, and made their way to the gates of Lafayette, and strolled together, admiring the graves."

It's easy to get lost in Mom's stories. I grew up with them, and sure, the tales she told me before bedtime were usually less morbid than these. But I love to hear her talk.

Now she comes to a stop in front of one of the crypts.

"And at some point, the couple realized that the young woman had stopped walking and was looking mournfully at one of the graves. And so they went to her, and asked, 'Do you know someone? Is that where they're buried?'

"And the woman smiled, and pointed at the grave . . ."

Mom reaches almost absently for the door of the crypt.

"And she said, 'This one's mine.'"

Chills race over my skin, and Jacob folds his arms and tries to look like he's not totally freaked out as Mom says, "The couple followed her gaze, and saw the name on the stone was *Annabelle*. And by the time they looked back at the young woman, she was gone."

Mom's hand still lingers in the air, as if reaching for the grave. I snap a photo before her fingers fall away, and I know, even before I've finished the roll, that shot will be my favorite one.

Dad steps up beside Mom.

"Some ghost stories are like gossip," he says, taking up his role as the skeptical scholar. "Passed from person to person. Who knows if they're true? But the next graveyard is home to something far more . . . *tangible*."

"Oh joy," says Jacob as the cameras cut off and Mom says it's time to head to St. Roch.

She's practically bouncing by the time we get there, as if this is the ride she's been waiting for.

From the outside, St. Roch seems like a pretty normal graveyard, which is a thing I never used to say. I hadn't exactly seen many graveyards before my parents decided to become the Inspecters. But in our brief time as a family of traveling paranormal investigators, I've walked through miles of bones and cemeteries large enough to need street signs, been pushed off crypts, fallen through crumbling bodies, and even climbed into an open grave.

"And that's not even counting the five places we've been today," says Jacob.

Mom grabs my hand and pulls me through the gate, and I feel the usual hush of unhaunted places. Or at least, *less* haunted ones.

I look around at the rows of stone monuments and crypts, wondering what the big deal is.

And then we enter the chapel.

"Oh sweet holy no," says Jacob at my side.

"What am I looking at?" I ask, even though I'm not sure I want to know.

It *looks* like a room full of body parts. Hands and feet. *Eyes* and *teeth*.

There are legs tacked up on the walls, a pile of crutches on the floor. An arm hangs over the table, and looks like it's waving at me. It takes me a second to realize that the body parts aren't real, that they're made of plastic, and plaster, and chipping paint.

My stomach churns.

"St. Roch," announces Mom. "Patron saint of good health. Unofficial recipient of used prosthetics."

A breeze blows through the chapel, and an artificial knee creaks.

"Some are symbolic," explains Mom. "A hand, for someone with carpal tunnel. A knee, for someone whose joints ache. But others are given in thanks. People bring them here when they don't need them anymore."

I stare at the shrine. A glass eye stares back, one wide blue iris fogging with age.

This place isn't haunted.

It's just really freaking creepy.

I back out of the chapel to give the film crew room, because the space is small, and because I really don't want to be surrounded by body parts, even if they're not real.

Jacob and I wander up the path, surveying graves with names like Bartholomew Jones, and Richard Churnell III, and Eliza Harrington Clark. Names that sound like something out of history, a play.

My parents' voices rise and fall from the chapel, following us like a breeze. Jacob scales a crypt and steps from roof to roof, as if he's playing hopscotch.

Thunder rolls through, the low clouds dark with the promise of more rain, and I can barely feel the Veil beyond the humid air.

And for a moment, I feel myself loosen, unwind.

And then I look around, and realize that unlike St. Louis No. 1 or Lafayette, there are no swells of tourists here right now, no groups clustered around the tombs.

The graveyard is empty around us.

And I remember Lara's warning.

Stay with your parents . . . Don't wander off.

"Jacob," I say softly.

But when I look up and scan the crypt rooftops, he's not there. My pulse picks up, my hand going to the pendant at my throat.

"Jacob!" I call, louder now.

Something moves at the edge of my vision, and I spin, already lifting the mirror when I see his superhero shirt, his messy blond hair.

"What?" he asks, cringing back from my pendant. "Can you put that away?"

I sag in relief. "Yeah," I say, a little shaky. "Sure."

We start back toward the morbid chapel and its offerings

of hands, and eyes, and teeth. And halfway there, the air changes.

At first I think it's just the storm. Maybe the sudden cold, the way all the wind drops out of the world, the eerie quiet, is just normal.

But I know it's not.

I've felt this way before.

On the platform in Paris.

In the séance room in the hotel.

And the only word I have for it is *wrong*.

Something is very, very wrong.

I look around, but I don't see anything strange.

I lift the camera to my eye and scan the cemetery again, peering through the viewfinder.

All I see are graves.

And then something steps between them.

In the viewfinder, it's . . . nothing. A void. A solid dark. A patch as black as unexposed film, just like I saw at the Place d'Armes.

When I lower the camera, the darkness has a shape.

Arms and legs in a black suit, a broad-brimmed hat low on its face, which isn't a face at all but a bone-white mask, black pools where there should be eyes. That mouth, set into a rictus grin.

The Emissary of Death holds out its hand, gloved fingers uncurling toward me.

"Cassidy Blake," it says in a voice like a rattle, a whisper, a wheeze.

"We have found you."

CHAPTER ELEVEN

"C assidy, run!" shouts Jacob.

But I can't.

When I try, it's like dragging my arms and legs through icy water. And when I try to breathe, I taste the river in my throat.

My feet are stuck to the ground, my eyes locked on the Emissary, and I don't know if it's fear or some kind of spell, but I can't speak, can't move. It's all I can do to grip the camera in my hands. The *camera*. My fingers scramble numbly, and I finally bring the camera up, turning it toward the advancing figure.

I hit the flash.

If the Emissary were a ghost, it would stop, stunned by the sudden burst of light. But the Emissary doesn't stop. It doesn't even flinch. It just keeps moving toward me, those long thin legs covering too much ground with every stride.

Jacob is still shouting, but I can barely hear him. The

world has gone cotton quiet. The only sounds that get through are my pulse and the too-heavy steps of the Emissary walking toward me.

"Once, you stole from us," it says, and the words wrap around me like water.

I feel like I'm in the river again, the cold leaching all the strength from my limbs.

"Once, you fled."

It reaches up for its mask, and I feel myself tipping forward, into the dark. The Emissary hooks one gloved finger under the bone mask, begins to lift its face away, when Jacob appears, all flailing limbs.

"Get away from my friend!" Jacob shouts, flinging himself at the Emissary. But Jacob goes straight through, and hits the ground on the other side. He collapses, shivering as if doused in cold water. His hair hangs wet around his face, and he spits a mouthful of river water onto the grass.

Jacob, I mouth his name.

The Emissary doesn't even seem to notice.

Its bottomless black eyes stay on me.

I manage a single backward stumble, clawing at my necklace. I hold up the mirror pendant like a too-small shield between me and the skeletal thing striding toward me. I force air into my lungs, and speak.

"Look and listen," I say, voice shaking. "See and know. This is what you are!"

But we're not in the Veil.

And the Emissary, whatever it is, is not a ghost.

It looks straight past the mirror at me, then closes its gloved hand around the pendant and tugs it free. The cord snaps, and the Emissary flings the mirror away. It hits a gravestone, and I hear the splinter of glass before the world is blotted out again by the Emissary's voice.

"We have found you," it says, *"and we will return you to the dark."*

It reaches forward, and I know that if it gets its hands on me, I will never get away. I know, but my legs are still like blocks of ice.

I shuffle backward again, make it a few clumsy steps before the ground changes beneath my feet, from gravel to stone, and a wall comes up against my back. A crypt, old and crumbling.

There's nowhere to run.

Jacob struggles to his feet, still looking damp, and dazed, and gray, and even if he were solid enough to fight, he wouldn't reach me in time.

The Emissary steps closer, and I resist the urge to close my eyes.

There's nowhere to run, but I won't hide.

I look up, into that skull face, those empty eyes, as it reaches out, gloved fingers skimming the air in front of my chest, carrying the touch of ice, and cold air, and deep shadow, as its other hand goes to its mask.

"*Cassidy Blake,*" says the Emissary, in its whispering way, "*come with—*"

Something shatters against the Emissary's hat.

A roof tile.

I look at Jacob, but he's still struggling to his feet.

And then a voice from the crypt over my head. A prim, English voice.

"Back off, reaper. She's not going anywhere with *you*."

The Emissary looks up, and so do I, and there's Lara Chowdhury standing on the crypt roof, dressed in a pair of shorts, a gray blouse, and a bright red backpack.

I'm still trying to figure out *how* she's there—*if* she's there—when she disappears, jumping down from the crypt and out of sight.

Maybe she thought the Emissary would follow her, but it doesn't.

"Lara?" I shout as the Emissary turns its focus back on me.

"Cassidy," she says from the other side of the crypt. "You might want to get out of the way."

The rotting tomb gives a violent groan against my back, and I realize what she's doing. I lunge out of the way, just before the old crypt sways, and splits, and topples forward.

It doesn't crush the Emissary, exactly. I don't think it's the kind of thing that *can* be crushed.

But the fall kicks up a lot of dust and debris, a thin gray cover. I hold my breath, trying not to inhale. A hand closes around my wrist, and I jump, stifling a shout, but it's just Lara. Impossible, amazing Lara. Who's really here.

"How are you here?" I ask, almost choking on crypt dust. "Where did you—"

"Questions later," she says briskly. "Right now, *run*."

I stumble, bending to scoop up my pendant from the

weedy base of a grave, grimacing when I see the mirror is broken—not just splintered, but shattered. I pocket it as Lara pulls me up again and pushes me toward the gates.

Jacob staggers after us, still looking shaken and damp. "Are you okay?" I ask him.

"Zero out of ten," he says with a shiver. "Do not recommend letting that thing touch you."

"Less talk, more flee," snaps Lara.

My ears are still ringing from the strange quiet that surrounds the Emissary, but as we near the graveyard gates, I swear I hear music. Not the eerie melody of the Veil but the high whine of a trumpet, followed by horns and a saxophone.

And then we hit the exit of St. Roch and I look up, and see a *parade*.

A very slow-moving parade. Cars crawl forward, and people walk on foot, some all in black and others in white, some holding flowers and others umbrellas. A marching band is staggered through the group like beads on a chain, gold instruments gleaming, as jazz rises through the street. And something moves at the center of it all, carried on either side by a pair of men.

It's a *casket*.

And this, I realize, isn't a parade.

It's a *funeral*.

Lara pulls me straight toward it.

We duck and weave through the slow-moving sea, slip through a gap between a drum and a horn, a pair of women in feathered Sunday hats and a carriage horse, tumbling out on the other side of the street.

The procession stretches as far as I can see.

"That's a lot of life and death," says Lara, pulling me down behind a car, "which is good cover. It should confuse the Emissary, at least for a while."

We crouch low, the three of us, and then Lara looks at me and the first thing she says, *really* says to me, is "I told you not to wander." And then she scowls at Jacob. "Honestly, how hard is it to keep her safe?"

"I'd like to see *you* try!"

Jacob finally looks like himself again, his blond hair dry and his color back (well, as much as it ever is).

Lara clucks her tongue and lifts her own mirror pendant, angling it over her shoulder, so she can see past the parade to the cemetery gates.

I reach for my mirror before remembering it's broken. My hand hovers as if it doesn't know what to do, before dropping onto my camera.

"Do you see it?" I ask, shifting so I can look, too.

The air lurches in my chest as the Emissary appears at the mouth of the cemetery. It pauses under the wrought-iron arch of St. Roch, head swiveling from side to side as it searches for us. For me.

And then it disappears, sliding apart like smoke.

"It's gone," I whisper.

"For now," says Lara, voicing the part I didn't want to think about. The Emissary came out of nowhere. It vanished into nowhere. Which means it could be anywhere.

We sag back against the car, waiting for the procession to pass.

"Lara," I say. "*How* did you get here?"

"I took a plane," she says, as if *that's* the part that needed explaining. "I was at the airport, and my parents' flight had already taken off. As you know, I was meant to go home, but I got to thinking, you are rather out of your element, and I have always wanted to see New Orleans—the Society of the Black Cat and all—so I changed the ticket."

"You just . . . changed the ticket?"

"Booked a layover, actually. It's not that hard. Did it all on my phone. I know my parents' credit card details. And it's a short flight from Chicago to New Orleans."

Even Jacob looks impressed.

"It will be a while before my parents check in with me," she says, "and I couldn't expect you to handle an Emissary on your own, so—"

I pull her into a hug.

Lara stiffens a little, clearly unused to the affection. But she doesn't pull away.

"Thank you," I say, squeezing her tight.

She pats my arm and looks over her shoulder. "We should go."

She's right. The music is fading, the funeral moving on and taking our cover with it.

"How did you even find me?" I ask as we get to our feet.

"In-betweeners stick together," Lara says, poking me in the chest. And I get what she's saying. There's a thread— not a physical one, but just as real—that runs between us. Like a compass pointing north. Which reminds me, for a second, of the weird feeling I had in Metairie Cemetery, that push-pull I felt, and I'm about to ask Lara if she knows what it is when a voice cuts across the road.

"Cassidy Blake!" snaps Mom.

The funeral procession is gone. The street is empty again, and my mother storms across it.

"How many times have we talked about wandering off during a— Oh my, Lara? Is that you?"

"Hello, Mrs. Blake."

"Sorry!" I say. "I wanted to see the parade. Or funeral, or whatever that was. And I ran into Lara!"

Lara shoots me a look. "What she means is, we talked about meeting up, and she told me where you all were."

Mom blinks. "Yes, but what on earth are you doing here?"

Lara's smile widens. "Would you believe, I was in the area? My aunt lives in the Quarter."

"Mrs. Weathershire?" asks Mom, remembering our host in Scotland.

"Oh, no, um, different aunt," Lara fumbles, and now it's my turn to give *her* a look. "She's been inviting me for months to come and visit, and when Cassidy told me you were here, too, it was just too perfect."

"Yes," says Mom slowly, "what are the odds?"

"She'll never believe that," says Jacob, but Lara Chowdhury has a power over grown-ups. I don't know if it's her English accent or her perfect posture, the fact that her black hair is always perfectly braided, her clothes clean and pressed, while I always look like I was just caught in a storm—but everyone treats *her* like an adult.

"Anyway," says Lara, "I know you're busy filming, but could Cassidy and I hang out for a bit?"

Mom blinks. "Well, yes, of course, but—" She looks up and down the street. "Is your aunt here with you?"

"Oh, she's at work right now, but we'll be careful."

Mom hesitates, clearly torn between the fact that I'm always getting into trouble, and the knowledge that I've made a friend.

Jacob clears his throat.

A *living* friend, I amend.

Mom looks back at St. Roch. "Well, we *are* almost done for the day . . ."

"Great," I say as Lara tugs me down the curb. "We'll meet you back at the hotel!"

"All . . . all right," says Mom, sounding a bit nervous. "But I want you back *before* it gets dark."

"Of course, Mrs. Blake," says Lara with a perfect smile, pulling me around the corner.

As soon as we're out of sight, Lara takes out her phone. A map of New Orleans fills the screen. "The trick with grown-ups," she says, setting off down the block, "is not to give them time to think."

She's always been a fast walker, and I have to jog to keep up.

"Where are we going?" I ask.

"Isn't it obvious?" she says. "We're going to find the Society."

PART THREE

THE SOCIETY OF THE BLACK CAT

CHAPTER TWELVE

Lara moves like a girl on a mission.

I mean, we *are* on a mission, but she always walks this way. Like she knows where she's going. Even when it turns out she doesn't.

"I thought you didn't know where the Society was," I call out, struggling to keep up.

"I don't," she says, readjusting her red backpack. "But it's a secret society dedicated to the paranormal, so there must be *some* kind of sign."

I look around at the placards in store windows advertising palm readings and tarot, voodoo and vampire tours. This city has plenty of signs, but as far as I can tell, none of them are for the Society.

Lara finally slows, and stops. "If I were running a paranormal society—and someday I will—I would put that sign somewhere other paranormal people would see it." She turns back toward me with a meaningful look.

"Like the Veil," I say, catching on.

"Precisely."

Lara turns on her heel, reaching for the curtain.

Jacob and I follow.

The air splits open, and I feel the now-familiar rush of cold, the momentary sense of falling, before the world comes back, grayer and stranger than it was before.

So does that weird double vision, the sense that I'm standing in multiple places at once—or multiple versions of the same place. One second smoke fills my vision, carrying the searing scent of fire. The next, I see people walk arm in arm on a sunny day. Jazz pours through the streets, along with laughter, and shouting, and a far-off siren's wail.

"Well, that's disconcerting," says Lara, closing one eye and then the other as she tries to focus. She cups her palm against one eye like a patch and sets off walking. We pass long cars, and carriage horses, and a group of men in oversized suits. Fire engulfs one balcony, and on the next, a couple dances.

I press my hand to my chest, trying to stifle the blue-white light. "I thought you said to stay *out* of the Veil."

"I did," says Lara, turning her backpack around so it's

on her front, dousing her own reddish light. "But things have gotten decidedly more dire. So we'll just have to be quick. In and out. Which would be easier if we knew where to start," she goes on, talking half to herself. "Let's see, the Society's been around for ages, so chances are it'll be in the oldest part of the Quarter."

We head to Jackson Square, which seems like a good place to start.

Gone are the performers, the men and women selling trinkets on pop-up tables. But the square is crowded with people, some of them ghosts and others just part of the background, like set dressing in someone else's play.

It's easy to tell the difference.

The ghosts look solid. Human. Real. The others look and move like phantoms. It's like the difference between rocks and tissue paper.

I jump back as a few spectral firemen rush by, carrying buckets of water. One second they're there, the next, gone, replaced by a pair playing saxophones in the shade.

A ghost leans against a post nearby, his head bowed and his boot thumping in time with the music, but that's not what catches my eye.

No, what I see is the hatchet resting on his shoulder.

Jacob sees it, too.

The Axeman of New Orleans.

"Nope," he says, steering me away.

Voices go up from the center of the square, and my stomach drops when I see an execution block. I'm grateful when Lara grumbles, "No, it's not here," and sets off down a side street.

Jacob and I follow, but ahead of us, Lara starts to look unsteady on her feet. She braces herself against a doorway, as if dizzy.

"Are you okay?" I ask.

"I'm fine," she says, sounding like she's about to faint.

"How long can you hold your breath?"

She frowns. "What?"

"I mean, here in the Veil, when I stay too long, it feels like I'm running out of air."

"Oh, yes, that. To be honest, I never stay that long."

Of course. Lara Chowdhury doesn't wander. She doesn't go for long dips in the Veil. Doesn't make a splash.

"We need to go," I tell her.

"Not until we find it." She rubs her eyes. "It has to be here somewhere."

I look around, hoping to find a sign. But then I remember, I already found one. I pull out my phone.

"Cassidy," says Lara. "I'm quite sure there's no cell service here."

But I'm not trying to make a call. I pull up the photo I took of the black cat. It was standing in front of a shop called Thread & Bone. A number *13* was mounted in iron over the door. I look around to get my bearings, and set off.

Lara stumbles after me. "Where are you going?"

"Following a clue." I turn the corner, and nearly collide with a pair of women in giant, old-fashioned dresses.

"Goodness," says one.

"How rude," scorns the other.

I offer a quick sorry, and keep going. The store was around here somewhere. I remember it. Every road in the Quarter kind of looks the same, and just a little different. I thought the store was on Bourbon—or was it Royal?

Lara catches up and looks at the photo on my screen.

"A cat?" she says incredulously. "This is New Orleans.

Do you have any idea how many black cats there are in this city?"

I know. But I also know that it's our only lead, and maybe, just maybe . . . I turn onto a street called Dauphine. And there it is.

Thread & Bone.

Or at least, a version of it.

The shop I saw yesterday had a beaded curtain instead of a door, and the sign was newer. The one here in the Veil is an older version.

Unfortunately, it also appears to be a normal one.

Normal for the Veil anyway, which means it's just as faded and gray as the other storefronts. There's no shining beacon, no tracery of light, nothing to say: *Here you are!* or *Congratulations! You found the Society of the Black Cat.*

Lara and Jacob catch up, and they stand beside me, staring at the shop.

"Well, that was a waste," says Lara, winded.

My heart sinks, and I wish for once things could just be simple. I rock back on my heels as Jacob marches past us and up to the shop.

"What are you do—" I start, but then he reaches for the

doorknob, and there's a giant *crack*, and for an instant the world goes *white*.

A giant, staticky buzz fills the air, and Jacob shoots backward several feet, landing in the middle of the street. A ghostly carriage veers, the horse rearing, as Jacob groans out an "Ow."

"Jacob!" I shout, rushing toward him.

"I'm fine," he mutters, smoke wafting off his clothes as he gets to his feet.

"What *was* that?" I ask.

"That," says Lara, hands on her hips, "is promising."

She approaches the door.

"Be careful," I hiss as her hand hovers over the metal knob. She swipes a fingertip across the handle, and pulls back as if singed.

Then she spins on her heel and smiles. "It's warded!" she says.

Jacob folds his arms. "Like the herbs and stuff designed to repel ghosts?"

"Yes and no," she says. "This ward is *much* stronger. If I had to guess, it's designed to repel anyone without an invitation." She turns to me. "Which means you were right."

And before I can savor those words, Lara's already reaching for the curtain. She vanishes through the Veil, and I take Jacob's hand and follow, past the rush of cold and into a cloud of heat as my feet settle back on the ground, the real world rushing to catch up.

We're standing in front of the Thread & Bone. Only now, the door is gone, replaced by a red beaded curtain, and the sign has been touched up, and there, on the sidewalk, is a black cat.

Not just any black cat, but the one I saw yesterday, with the amethyst eyes. The cat looks up at us. If it's surprised to see two girls and a ghost step out of the Veil and into the land of the living, it doesn't show it.

It just yawns and stretches, tail twitching side to side.

I shoot Lara a look that says, *See?*

She rolls her eyes and says, "Yes, all right," as the black cat turns and slips through the beaded curtain into the shop. It stops on the other side, looking back as if to say, *Follow me.*

And we do.

CHAPTER THIRTEEN

The Thread & Bone is a voodoo shop.

Or at least, it's made to look like one. Every inch of space is covered in candles and crystals and charms. Silk scarves, and jars of oil. It looks like something out of Diagon Alley, and I have to remind myself that Harry Potter is fantasy, and this is real. Jacob follows me, holding his breath, but when he finally inhales, a small, questing sniff, he sighs with relief.

No spirit repellents inside.

Just a shelf of candles, tied with different colored ribbons. Dolls made of sticks and blank cloth. Bundles of unlit incense. A bowl of blue-and-white beads.

I slow down to look at a painting of a thin man standing at a crossroads. It reminds me of the Two of Swords, and I'm just about to step closer when I hear Lara say, "That's it!"

We find her near the back of the shop, standing in front of a black-curtained doorway. There's a symbol stitched into the dark cloth, an ornate *S*, set over a starburst.

Lara pulls a business card from her pocket and holds it up. The same symbol is pressed into the front. I recognize it, too, from the card that came with my sachets of sage and salt back in Paris.

The Society of the Black Cat.

My pulse picks up, and Lara looks almost giddy, but she takes a moment to smooth her shirt and run a hand over her braid. And then she reaches for the black curtain, ready to pull it aside, as if it were the Veil.

"You can't go in there."

We all jump, turning toward the voice.

There's a young woman sitting behind the shop counter.

I swear she wasn't there before. Or maybe she was just sitting so still, we didn't notice her. But it seems hard not to notice her. She's maybe twenty, white, with hair so blond it's practically silver. It's shaved on one side, and tumbles like a wave down the other.

"Can I help you find something?" she asks.

Lara steps up, taking control.

"We're here to see the Society."

"Society?" the girl says, arching a brow. Jacob and I exchange a look, wondering if we're in the right place. But Lara doesn't flinch.

"Of the Black Cat," Lara says.

The girl stares at us blankly. The cat from outside jumps up onto the glass counter and purrs, its purple eyes locked on us. "This black cat?" asks the girl, running her hand over its fur.

Lara huffs. "No. Look—"

"Where are your parents?"

That tips Lara over the edge. "*My* parents are on their way to South America, and Cassidy's are currently in one of your city's forty-two graveyards filming a show on the paranormal—"

"Well, *that* sounds like fun!"

"And we're *here*, because we need the Society's help, and don't tell me it's not here because it was warded in the Veil, and Cassidy followed the cat, and I saw the symbol on the curtain, and it's the same as the one on my card."

Lara's breathless by the time she slaps the business card down on the counter.

The girl lifts it gingerly, but the airy confusion is gone, replaced by a mischievous grin. "How did you get this?"

"My great-uncle was a member."

"But you're not."

"A technicality," says Lara through gritted teeth. "Some ageist wording in the bylaws, but I'm working on it. You see, Cassidy and I, we're in-betweeners."

"Veil-walkers! Fascinating," the girl says, leaning forward on her elbows. "We don't have any of those right now. We used to have one, but he . . ." She trails off.

"Died?" I ask nervously.

"Goodness, no," she says brightly. "He moved to Portland. There are no ghosts in Portland. Odd quirk in the landscape or somethi—"

"So this *is* the Society?" interrupts Lara.

"Oh yeah," says the girl, waving her hand. "But you know, we have to be careful. Can't go around telling everyone who wanders in."

Jacob has drifted toward the counter, and the cat.

"This is Amethyst, by the way," the girl says. "Mascot and protector."

"Protector of what?" I ask.

She shrugs. "People. Cats are drawn to the supernatural. They're often seen as omens, portents of danger, but they're also amulets against it. Cats make excellent protectors. They're very brave," she adds, scratching Amethyst behind the ears.

I picture Grim, sitting like a bread loaf in a pool of sun. Once, a bug landed near him, and instead of pouncing on it, he got up and walked away.

"And sensitive," she says, scratching between the cat's ears. "They can sense trouble."

Jacob wiggles his fingers in front of the cat's face.

The girl behind the counter shoots him a look. "Please don't antagonize my cat."

Her attention flicks back to us, but Jacob stares at her, his eyes wide as marbles.

"Cassidy," he hisses under his breath, "I think she can . . ."

"See you," finishes the girl. "Yes. I wouldn't be much of a medium if I couldn't see ghosts."

Jacob sucks in a breath. His eyes narrow to slits. "How many fingers am I holding up?" he asks.

"Two."

He gasps. "No one has ever been able to see me."

"I've *always* been able to see you," I say, hurt.

"So have I," adds Lara, sounding more annoyed than wounded.

"I meant normal people," he shoots back.

"Oh, no normal people here," says the girl with a laugh. "In-betweeners," she muses, looking at me and Lara. "And you're friends with this ghost? I didn't think in-betweeners were fond of spirits."

"We're not," says Lara.

"He's different," I explain.

Jacob puffs up his chest a little.

The medium studies him. "Yes," she says. "I think he is." She addresses Jacob directly. "You look a little . . . corporeal for a ghost."

"Why, thank you," says Jacob.

"It's not a compliment," she says, attention flicking back to me and Lara. "I'm Philippa, by the way. Now, why do you want to see the Society?"

Lara looks at me. I clear my throat.

"I'm being chased by a missionary of Death."

"Emissary," corrects Lara.

"Oh my," says Philippa. "That sounds serious. Hold on."

She rings a bell, and a few moments later, two people pass through the curtain at the back of the shop.
A middle-aged Black woman wearing pink glasses, and a
younger white man with a shock of black hair. His wid-
ow's peak makes him look like he belongs in a vampire
story.

"We have guests," Philippa tells them brightly. "Veil-
walkers! Or, what did you call it, in-betweeners? Anyway,
this is Cassidy and Lara."

Lara and I exchange a look.

We never said our names.

Jacob clears his throat, and Philippa adds, "Oh yes,
sorry, and Jacob, their incorporeal friend. This," she says,
nodding at the woman, "is the current president of the
Society, Renée. And this is Michael, our specialist in wards
and charms. I'm afraid our historian is out."

"Lara Chowdhury," says Renée, looking her up and
down. "I've received your letters."

"And yet you still haven't granted me membership—"

"Not why we're here," I say impatiently.

Renée turns her attention to me. "Yes, what brings you to the Society?"

"We need help," I say. "I'm being hunted by an Emissary."

Renée frowns. "Indeed," she says soberly. "Well then, come on back."

She gestures to Michael, who pulls the curtain aside. Lara and I step through, out of the shop and into a narrow room. Jacob tries to follow us, but when he reaches the curtain, he begins to sniffle and sneeze. And when he tries to come through anyway, he . . . bounces off. Like there's a plate of glass there instead of an open doorway.

He rubs his forehead.

"Oh yes," calls Philippa, "I'm afraid that room is warded."

Jacob looks from me, to Lara, to the floor, and shoves his hands in his pockets. "I guess I'll just wait out here, then," he says, and I swear the temperature drops a little with his mood.

"I'll be back soon," I tell Jacob.

Philippa pats a stool by the counter. "Come and sit with me," she says. "I'll show you a fun trick."

Jacob frowns a little, and I realize there's never been a place I've gone that he couldn't follow. But he turns away, and the last thing I see is his back before the curtain falls shut between us.

CHAPTER FOURTEEN

The Society room is filled with books.

Shelves run along every wall, interrupted only by sofas and chairs, and a small round table in the center. It feels a little like a library, and a little like an office, and a little like the séance room in Muriel's, just as cluttered but far less ominous.

It's so quiet in here, and it takes me a second to realize it's because of the Veil. Or rather, the absence of it. Ever since I got to New Orleans, the other side has been a crush against my senses. But here, in the back room of the Thread & Bone, the Veil drops away, taking the whispers and the music with it.

"I thought the Society would be . . ." Lara turns in a circle. "Bigger."

"Looks can be deceiving," says Renée with a shrug. "Have a seat."

I sit cross-legged on an ottoman, while Lara chooses a

high-backed chair. Her legs don't even reach the ground, and yet somehow she still looks dignified. Michael leans against the bookshelves, while Renée stands, arms folded, studying us behind her pink glasses.

"In-betweeners," she muses. "You're both so young."

"Age is a number," replies Lara briskly, "as I've said in my letters."

"Yes, as you've said. And as I've said, Miss Chowdhury, the Society's restrictions on age are in place for a reason."

"Well, it's a foolish reason, if you ask me."

"I'm sorry," I say, "can we please focus on the thing with the skull-face mask that keeps trying to kill me?"

"It's not trying to kill you," says Renée.

"Not in the strictest sense," adds Michael, pulling a book from the shelf. "It's trying to undo the fact that you lived."

Somehow, that isn't very comforting.

"Okay," I say, "well, how do I make it *stop*?"

Michael flips through the book, then shakes his head. "We don't know much about Emissaries," he says. "They really only come after Veil-walkers, or in-betweeners, as you say. And we haven't had one of those since—"

"Since he moved to Portland," says Lara, "yes, we heard."

"And he didn't make any notes," says Michael, sliding the book back onto the shelf.

"Okay," I say, resisting the urge to put my head in my hands. "So you have no idea what I'm supposed to do?"

"I didn't say that," replies Michael.

"*We* don't know enough," says Renée. "But the other members might."

I look around the tiny room. "There are more?"

Renée smiles and spreads her hands. "This is the oldest branch of the Society," she says. "And former members tend to stick around."

Former members.

Ghosts.

I think of Lara's uncle, lingering in their living room even though he wasn't trapped there, even though he could have passed on. Staying behind because he wanted to help.

"There are a few in-betweeners in the bunch," says Michael. "Maybe one of them will know."

Lara and I exchange a look. We have to go back into the Veil.

She holds out her hand. But I hesitate.

"What if the Emissary is waiting there?" I say.

"This is the Society, Miss Blake," says Renée. "It's warded a dozen different ways. Think of our Veil as a vault. Somewhere very safe."

Safe.

If I've learned anything over the past couple of weeks, it's that grown-ups throw around that word way too much. But I did see the shop repel Jacob. And I don't have much choice.

I take Lara's hand, and together we reach for the Veil, and even though it hasn't been loud or pushy, it's right there, waiting beneath my fingers. I pull the curtain aside and hold my breath against the moment of dark, the flush of cold, the feel of falling.

And then we're back.

Lara looks a little flushed, and I wonder what she feels when she crosses over. But I know it's not the time to ask.

I look around for Jacob before remembering he isn't there.

It feels wrong, going through the Veil without him.

Like a piece of me is missing.

As for the Society room, it looks the same. A little faded, perhaps, and even more cluttered. No sign of Renée or Michael, of course, but we're not alone.

A girl my age, and just as pale, with a crown of dark hair and a yellow sundress, leans against the wall, twisting a Rubik's Cube.

A middle-aged man in a bow tie is napping on a sofa, while an ancient woman with wild gray curls sits beside him, fingers folded over a cane and staring at the wall as if it were a window.

An older Black man with a mustache looks up from his book.

A young white woman with a pixie cut wanders through the room, gripping a mug of coffee that reads THINK OF A NUMBER.

"Oh, hello!" she says, as if the sight of two new in-betweeners is perfectly normal.

She pokes a finger toward the blue-white light in my chest, and I pull away on instinct.

She cackles.

"A Veil-walker." She looks from me to Lara. "Two of them! What a Wednesday! Is it Wednesday? It's so easy to lose track."

"Does it matter?" asks the girl with the Rubik's Cube, her accent pure Louisiana, syrup and sweet.

"Time always matters," says the older man with the book.

"Until it doesn't," says the ancient woman.

"Look at us, chattering away," says the woman with the coffee mug. "Where are my manners? I'm Agatha."

Lara and I introduce ourselves.

"Sit, sit," says Agatha, "make yourselves comfortable."

There's not a lot of space, but we perch on the edge of the dusty furniture.

"That's Theodore," Agatha says, gesturing at the old man with the book. "Hazel," she says, nodding at the girl with the sundress and the Rubik's Cube. "Charles—wake up, Charles!" she shouts toward the napping man with

155

the bow tie. "And Magnolia," she finishes, nodding to the ancient woman bowed over her cane.

"Are—were you all in-betweeners?" I ask.

"Goodness no. And we use the present tense here, child. Makes us feel a bit more up to speed. Hazel and I are mediums." The girl's gaze flicks up from the Rubik's Cube. "Charles—somebody wake him up?—is a historian. Magnolia handles the voodoo, and Theodore here, he is—or, sorry, Theo, I do have to say *was*—a Veil-walker."

I look toward Theo's chest, where the light would have been. It's gone now, of course.

"And you all just stay here?" asks Lara.

"We're on shifts. Some of us are a bit more lively than others. But let's see, Harry and Renata are out patrolling, Lex was supposed to be shoring up the wards on the shop after *someone* tried to get in"—she raises a meaningful brow as she says it—"and knowing Sam, she's probably drinking gin and listening to jazz in the square." She takes a swig from the mug. "And what about you two? You're awfully young to be Society members."

Hazel clears her throat. She doesn't look any older than us.

"Well, yes, but yours was a tragic end," Agatha tells her, and then examines me and Lara again. "You're not dead, though. Just visiting. So what can we do for you?"

Lara straightens to her full height, which is still a good inch below mine. "We're here to seek your guidance."

"No need to be so formal," says Agatha. "Just tell us the trouble."

Lara glances at me.

I swallow and say, "I'm being hunted by an Emissary."

For a second, no one says anything.

Hazel stares at me with wide, sad eyes, and the ancient woman, Magnolia, thumps her cane thoughtfully on the floor.

Agatha nods and says, "Right. Best tell us everything."

I do. I tell them about the stranger on the train platform in Paris. I tell them about the Place d'Armes and the séance, the skull in the stone and the voice in the dark, and what it said. I tell them about the close call in St. Roch, and when I'm done, the words hang in the air for a moment, like smoke.

And then the napping man, Charles, sighs and sits up.

"That's no good," he says, which feels like a bit of an understatement.

"The historian wakes!" scolds Agatha. "Honestly, Charles. This is a society, not a sunroom. Now, Theodore," she says, turning to the man with the book. The in-betweener. "Have you ever seen an Emissary?"

The old man with the mustache closes his book. "Only once. Gave me the shivers. Lucky it didn't see me. But we did lose another Veil-walker, didn't we? Some years back."

The historian, Charles, nods at the bookshelf. "Joanna Bent," he says. "She's gone on her way, but she made notes."

Hazel sets her Rubik's Cube aside and studies the books, fingers trailing over the spines before she pulls down a slim journal and turns through the pages.

"Dangerous things, Emissaries," says Theodore. "Like spotlights, scanning the dark."

Hazel clears her throat.

"'Death's Emissaries,'" she reads in her Southern drawl, "'are drawn to things out of place. To life in the presence of death, and death in the presence of life. To people who embody both.'"

"That's why they're so good at finding in-betweeners," says Lara. "We're life and death mixed up in one."

I shake my head. "But I don't get *why* they want to find us. In-betweeners have a purpose. We clear out the Veil. We send spirits on. Shouldn't Death be grateful?"

Agatha purses her lips. "I don't think Death cares about the dead. Think about what the Emissary said to you. 'You stole from us.' It was talking about your *life*. The ghosts in the Veil don't have lives anymore. Just look at the threads in our chests." She gestures to her own. "All the light's gone out. But you—"

I look down at the blue-white light glowing behind my ribs.

"That's what you stole, when you survived. That's what Death wants back."

None of this is making me feel any better. I wish Jacob were here. I think everything, as loudly as I can, and hope that he can hear me through the wards and the Veil.

I swallow and turn to Agatha. "Michael said the Emissary wants to undo the fact I lived. So if it catches me, it will—what?" A nervous sound escapes my throat. "Drown me?"

The members share a long look, a silent conversation, before Magnolia says, in a rasping voice, "It will take you back."

"Back where?" I ask. "To the Veil?"

"No," says Charles, now very much awake. "To the place beyond the Veil. To the other side."

My chest tightens. I feel dizzy.

"What are we supposed to do?" demands Lara, and I can hear the nervous energy seeping through her usual calm.

"Hide," says Hazel.

But we *can't*. "What good is hiding?" I snap, exasperated.

"Cassidy's right," says Agatha. "No sense in hiding from a thing like Death."

I look around, suddenly nervous.

"Don't worry," she adds. "Nothing can get into the Society, unless it's been invited in."

"I knew it," whispers Lara.

"Like a vampire," I say, because it's what Jacob would say if he were here.

Right about then, I start to realize another strange thing about this room.

Normally, time in the Veil is a ticking clock. If I spend

too long there, my head begins to swim, and I feel dizzy and lost. A reminder that even if I can move among the dead, I still belong to the land of the living.

And yet, I don't feel dizzy here.

I don't feel wrong, or out of place.

I feel . . . *safe*.

I wish I could stay here. But I know I can't.

"I'd avoid graveyards if I were you," says Hazel, taking up her Rubik's Cube. "Anywhere that's all living or all dead. Best stick to confusing places," she adds, "where the energy is as messy as yours."

"The good news," says Agatha, "is New Orleans is a perfect place to blend in."

I think of the funeral party, all that life surrounding death. The way the Emissary broke apart and disappeared. Maybe it got overwhelmed. Maybe.

But I can't hide forever. I'm tired of being scared, of seeing that skull face everywhere I look and every time I close my eyes.

"The Emissary will just keep coming, right? Until I kill it." I look around the table. "So how do you kill an Emissary of Death?"

"You can't," says Charles.

My heart sinks.

"You'll have to banish it," says Hazel.

"Mirrors don't work," I say, losing hope. "I've tried."

"No, they wouldn't," says Theodore. "An Emissary knows exactly what it is. And it's caught you, like a fish on a line. You won't get away, as long as it can reel you in."

"Great," I say, summoning as much of Jacob's sarcasm as I can.

"But," says Magnolia, holding up a withered finger. "With the right tools, you could cut the line."

Lara and I exchange a look. "How?" Lara asks.

A short debate breaks out between the members, first on whether it's possible, and then, when they agree that it is, on what we'll need to do it.

I can't exactly take notes in the Veil, but Lara has a scary good memory.

"And you're sure it will work?" I ask when the Society members have explained.

"It'll be dangerous," says Agatha, "but you're used to that by now, aren't you?"

We thank them for their time and help.

"Nonsense," she says, lifting her mug, "we enjoy the company."

"Good luck," adds Hazel as we reach for the curtain.

And I know we're going to need it.

CHAPTER FIFTEEN

Lara and I step back through the Veil.

A shiver, and a sigh, and then the Society room is warm and solid around us again. Michael and Renée are seated at the table, in the middle of a discussion with someone else, but they trail off when they see us.

"Never got used to that part," says Michael, gesturing to our sudden reappearance, but I'm staring past him, at the new arrival.

"Ah, yes," says Renée, gesturing to the man in the chair. "This is our current historian."

I stand there, mouth open.

Because the man in the chair is Lucas Dumont, our guide.

Surprise flashes across his face, but it only lasts a second.

"Actually," he says, rising to his feet, "we've already met. Admittedly, it was under *different* circumstances.

Cassidy . . ." He trails off, as if waiting for me to explain. Lara looks at me, too, and I realize that *they* haven't met.

"This is my parents' guide, Lucas," I explain.

"Ah, the paranormal show," says Renée. "Small world, isn't it?"

"Very," says Lucas, polishing his glasses. He nods at Lara. "And you are?"

"Lara Chowdhury," she says, standing even straighter. "Future member of the Society. And Cassidy's friend."

"I see," he says in his measured way. "And what exactly are *you* doing here, Miss Blake?"

I don't know if he expects me to tell him the whole story from almost-drowning to being an in-betweener to my current predicament, so I just say, "I'm kind of . . . being hunted."

"Emissary," says Renée, "nasty business."

"Were the others able to help?" asks Michael.

I try to drag my focus away from the fact that my parents' very skeptical historian is a member of a paranormal secret society. We're definitely going to have to talk about that later.

"Yes," says Lara. "I think we have a plan."

"Excellent," says Renée. "Who did you meet? Agatha? Theo?" She leads me and Lara back through the black curtain and into the brightly lit store. Jacob is sitting on a stool by the counter, having a staring contest with the cat and chatting with Philippa.

But he looks up as soon as I come through.

"Lucas Dumont is in the Society!" he announces.

"Yeah, I know," I say, nodding at the curtain as Michael and Lucas follow us out. "I guessed that when I saw him in there."

Jacob's shoulders slump. "Well, you weren't here to be surprised with me," he sulks, "so I had to save it." He hops down from the stool. "Well? What did you learn?"

"You couldn't hear me thinking?"

Jacob shakes his head. "No. It was just . . . quiet. Like white noise."

"That would be the warding," says Philippa, and I wonder, just for a second, if there's a way to ward my thoughts *all* the time.

Jacob scowls, reading my mind, and I say, a little too loudly, "Privacy is important!"

And even though Renée, Michael, and Lucas can't see Jacob, and it must look like I'm having a very tense discussion with empty air, they don't seem thrown. I guess it's probably not the strangest thing they've come across.

"We learned," explains Lara, "that Emissaries are drawn to those marked by life *and* death. That's how this one caught Cass's . . . scent."

This is the part where Jacob would usually make a joke, but he doesn't, and when I glance his way, he looks . . . pale, what little color he has draining out of his face.

"Was it because of me?" he whispers.

"What? Don't be silly," I say. "I'm the one who's an in-betweener."

"The Emissary must have caught your scent in Paris," says Lara. "And followed you here."

"What if it's me?" Jacob murmurs.

"It doesn't matter how it found me," I say. "What matters is that it's here, in New Orleans. And it's going to keep coming after me until we send it back. Or on. Or wherever Emissaries go when they aren't—"

"Listen to me!"

Jacob slams his hand down against the display case, and

I hear the crack, the splinter of glass. We all stop talking then and look, in shock, in horror, in surprise.

Before this, Jacob has turned pages and fogged windows. But this is the first time he's broken something.

He looks down through his palm at the cracking starburst in the glass, the damage spreading from the shape of his fist.

There's no triumph on his face, no glee, only fear.

"What if it's me?" he whispers again, as if he can barely get the words out. "What if I'm the reason it found you?" He looks from me to Lara and back. "You said Emissaries are drawn to people touched by life and death. But I'm literally haunting Cassidy. That has to make it easier to find her, that has to make her louder, or brighter, or . . ."

"*Jacob,*" says Lara sternly. "Listen to me very carefully. Emissaries are drawn to in-betweeners. We have a marker, a signature. But you, you throw the whole thing off. Because you are not supposed to be here, with her."

"I don't think that's making him feel better," I say as Jacob's head falls, but Lara pushes on.

"You are confusing, and wrong. You mess up the

balance. And you are probably the only reason Cassidy is still alive."

Jacob looks up, surprised. I look over at Lara, just as stunned.

"What do you mean?" he murmurs.

Lara makes an exasperated sound. "You're not normal, Jacob! You're a ghost, tied to a living girl, siphoning off her life force until you're strong enough to do things like put your hand through a glass display counter. You're probably throwing the entire Veil off balance every second you're still here. But you're also probably confusing the Emissary, and buying us time."

Jacob swallows, rubbing his knuckles. "Are you sure?"

"No," snaps Lara. "I'm not an expert in the long-term effects of ghost-human friendships. But I do believe that she's safer with you than without you. Now," she says, turning back toward the other members of the Society. "We're going to need some things from your store."

We lay the supplies out on the counter.

A handful of stones, to anchor the circle.

A ball of white string, to tether me to the living.

A bottle of scented oil, to purify, and to burn.

And a box of long wooden matches, to strike the flame.

Elements of creation, and destruction. Of life, and death. Give and take, as Lucas said as we were gathering up the items from around the store.

"I'm not sure how I feel about this," says Renée, watching us.

But we've explained the spell—is it a spell? I don't know what else to call it, and I'm kind of excited I get to do one, even if the only reason we get to do one is because I'm being chased by Death.

"It sounds like more of a ritual," says Jacob. "A summoning? No, what's the opposite of a summoning? A banishing?"

As far as I can tell, it *is* a kind of banishing spell. A way to sever the connection between the Emissary and me. The problem is, in order for it to work, we have to be in the same place. Which means we either have to go looking for Death, or wait for it to come to us.

"Oh, what are these?" Jacob points to a row of brightly colored pouches. "Do we need one?"

I pick up a pretty red pouch. It's a small, solid weight in my palm, and when I lift it to my nose, it smells . . . earthy. Damp. Like the woods after a storm.

"That," says Philippa, "is a gris-gris bag."

I look up. "What does it do?"

"All kinds of things. They're talismans. Some for protection, and others for luck, prosperity. That one, I believe, is for balance."

Balance. I think of the tarot card, the Two of Swords, the need to balance the scales.

"What's in it?" asks Jacob.

"Oh, a little of this, a little of that," says Philippa. "Let's see, that one has a crystal, and some herbs, nail clippings, hair, a bit of grave dirt."

I yelp and drop the bag, but Philippa catches it before it falls.

"Careful," she says, petting the bag. "You've got to treat them nice. Feed and water them . . ."

"What does it *eat*?" whispers Jacob as Philippa sets the pouch back on the shelf.

"Speaking of grave dirt," says Michael, producing a black pouch the size of a softball. "This should be enough."

I don't want to reach for the bundle, but I do, expecting to feel some terrible omen pass over me when it hits my hands. But it just feels like a bag of dirt.

I realize I can't pay for any of it—not unless they're willing to take a handful of international coins—but Renée waves me away. "The Society looks after its own."

We load the supplies into Lara's red backpack as Lucas polishes his glasses and says we really should be going. I wish I could stay here, in the safety of the shop, but he's right. It's getting late, and my parents will be waiting back at the hotel.

Jacob turns toward Philippa, who seems to be having a one-sided conversation with Amethyst the cat.

"Sorry," he says, "about the case."

She blinks, and looks up. "Things break," she says with a shrug, as if she's lost more than one display case to a moody spirit.

"Wait," says Michael, "that reminds me."

He takes two charms from a cabinet behind the counter. Smooth glass circles threaded onto cords. He hands one to Lara, presses the other into my palm. When I look down at the charm, I see a series of blue and white rings around a black dot.

It almost looks like an eye.

"An evil eye," confirms Michael. "It won't do much to *stop* an Emissary, but it might buy you some time. The charm's designed to break when someone wishes you ill. It should break when danger's near."

"Thank you," I say to Michael, pocketing the evil eye. And then I look at Renée, and Philippa. "Thank you for everything."

"Good luck," says Michael.

"Be careful," says Renée.

"Come back anytime," says Philippa brightly as Lucas leads us out.

CHAPTER SIXTEEN

The walk back to the hotel is weird.

Not the being-hunted-by-an-Emissary kind of weird. More the I-have-so-many-questions-I-don't-know-where-to-start kind of weird.

Jacob circles Lara, demanding to know every detail of the room beyond the shop curtain, while Lucas and I walk side by side, and I wait for him to say something, and he doesn't.

"So, are we going to talk about this?" I finally ask.

Lucas eyes me over his wire-framed glasses. "About what?"

"You're a member of the Society of the Black Cat!"

"I'm a historian."

"You're *their* historian. But you said you don't even believe in ghosts!"

Lucas slides his glasses from his face and begins to polish them again. "I believe what I said was that I prefer to focus on the history."

"Does he have any supernatural powers?" Jacob calls out. I ask the question, and Lucas scrunches his nose.

"Beyond an extreme dedication to research? No. I'm not a psychic, or a medium, or an in-betweener, as you say."

"Did you know that *I* was?"

He considers that a moment. "No. But when you spend as much time as I do around the . . . paranormally inclined, you do notice certain signs."

I look down at myself. "Like what?"

"The way you walk, for one, like you're always listening to something others don't hear. You're clearly sensitive to haunted spaces, you spend a fair amount of time talking to someone only you can see, and you have a way of disappearing rather suddenly."

I nod, considering. "Fair point. His name is Jacob, by the way. The one I'm talking to."

Jacob waves. "Hey. Jacob Ellis Hale," he says to Lucas, holding out his hand, "best friend, partner in crime, excellent taste in comics."

Of course, Lucas can't hear him, but I convey the message.

"I'm surprised you would allow yourself to be haunted," Lucas says as we turn onto Bourbon Street.

"It's unconventional," says Lara, "but he comes in handy now and then."

Jacob stares at Lara as if she just sprouted a second head. I have to admit, I'm pretty surprised, too. Up until today, the closest Lara's come to paying Jacob a compliment has been calling him Jacob instead of Ghost. Now, in the space of thirty minutes, she's been nice to him—twice.

"I clearly don't approve," she clarifies. "But I think we have bigger problems right now . . ." She trails off as we reach the hotel.

"Kardec," she says, reading the sign. "As in the French founder of Spiritism?"

"Precisely," says Lucas, sounding impressed.

"Wow," says Lara, surveying the lobby, "they really went with the theme."

"Wait till you see our room," says Jacob.

"Your parents are done filming for the day," Lucas tells me, "so I'll see you in the morning. Do stay safe, Cassidy. Lara."

"No ever says goodbye to me," mutters Jacob as Lucas turns to go.

"Wait!" I call out. I still have a dozen questions, but I choose to settle for the most important one. "You won't tell my parents, will you? About . . ." I gesture at us, at everything.

Lucas raises a brow and gives me a half smile. "Me? I'm just the guide."

We watch him leave, and I remember my first impression of Lucas Dumont, a skeptical scholar, just like Dad. I guess you never know.

"Do you think your dad is secretly a member of a paranormal society?" asks Jacob, and I snort.

"Doubtful," I say as we cross the lobby.

Halfway to the stairs, I notice the sign hanging on the door to the séance room.

OUR MASTER OF SPIRITS IS AWAY.
THE SÉANCE ROOM WILL BE CLOSED
UNTIL FURTHER NOTICE.
WE APOLOGIZE FOR THE INCONVENIENCE.

I wonder why he left.

"If I had to guess," says Jacob, "it probably had some-thing to do with *your* séance."

Oh. Right. The whole channeling-actual-Emissaries-of-Death-when-you-just-wanted-to-put-on-a-show. I can see how that would be upsetting.

Upstairs, Mom and Dad have changed out of their Inspecters outfits and into loose, summery clothes. Dad's even wearing *shorts.*

"Did you girls have fun?" asks Mom.

We make some noncommittal sounds, peppering in the word *yes.*

"What did you get up to?" asks Dad.

Well, I think, *we located a secret society dedicated to studying the paranormal, and we met its living members—your guide is one of them!—and then had a conference with some of its dead ones, and they helped us figure out how to banish the Emissary of Death that's chasing me and hopefully it works so I won't die. Again.*

"Not much," I say casually. "We just wandered around the Quarter."

I toss my camera onto the bed, and Lara leans her back-pack down against a chair. Her bag's not zipped all the way, and Grim wanders over and starts rooting around inside. He's almost got the pouch of grave dirt open when I realize what's happening. I rush over and scoop him up.

The last thing we need is the cat treating our spell supplies like a litter box.

Grim sighs in protest, and then goes limp in my arms, like a sack of, well, grave dirt. If grave dirt had lots of fur and a low, grudging purr.

I hoist him up and look into his sleepy green eyes.

"Are you my brave protector?" I ask.

Grim looks at me for a moment, and then opens his mouth wide, and for a second, I think he's displaying his rows of tiny sharp teeth. But then I realize it's just a yawn.

Punctuated by a burp.

Dad laughs, and I sigh and set the cat on the chair, where he promptly sinks into a puddle.

"Good thing you have me," says Jacob. "I'm pretty sure that cat is useless."

Grim twitches one ear, already asleep.

"Well, I don't know about you," says Mom, pulling the pens from her messy bun, "but Cemetery Day has made me famished! Shall we go find dinner?"

*   *   *

There's a kind of restaurant Dad calls a "hole in the wall."
I think it's supposed to mean a cozy little place, the kind
you only know about if someone's told you, or you've been
there before. Like the Society, but for food.

Tonight we eat in the Marigny, a neighborhood just
north of the Quarter. To get to the restaurant, we don't
have to step through an *actual* hole in the wall, but it's
pretty close. We go through a gate and down an overgrown
courtyard, across a threshold that looks like it was a wall
once, before someone knocked the center out.

But the food—the food is amazing.

Bowls of gumbo, and shrimp étouffée, jambalaya, and
other dishes with winding, musical names, full of heat
and spice.

I forget the one-bite rule and dig in, tasting everything.

Lara reaches out a fork and takes a dainty bite of each,
and despite the messy nature of the meal, she never spills
a spoonful or loses a grain of rice. I bet she could eat a
beignet dressed in black and never get a speck of powdered
sugar on her.

All through dinner, I keep the evil eye charm nestled in my

180

palm, bracing for trouble, jumping at the slightest scrape of a chair or strange angle of light. But Lara smiles and chats as if nothing's wrong. She's so good at pretending everything's okay. I watch her, wishing I was better at it. But it also makes me sad, that she has so much practice at it.

And even though we've only known each other a couple of weeks, having her here feels *right*.

Even Jacob has softened toward her, and more than once I catch him and Lara exchanging looks, not even murderous ones, but the kinds of glances that pass between friends.

It makes me feel happy, and full.

"I met my first ghost in London," Mom is saying to Lara. "When I was about your age. Not in the Tower, or in one of the graveyards, or anything like that. I was on a double-decker bus."

I sit forward, realizing I've never heard this story.

"He was just sitting there," Mom goes on, "looking out the window, waiting for his stop. He asked if I would hit the button, and I did, and he got up and walked away, and I called after him that I hoped he had a nice day. And my father looked at me and said, 'Who are you talking to?'"

Mom breaks into a smile. "The boy wasn't there, of course. Not anymore. And I've never *seen* a ghost like that since—but it was such a thrilling thing. Like a corner of my world had pulled away, revealing a whole new place."

I bite my lip, wishing that someday I could show her that other place, take her with me through the Veil.

"Is that why you write books?" asks Lara.

Mom sips her drink and hums a little, thinking. "You know, maybe it is. Stories have a way of making the world feel bigger, too."

Lara nods and looks down at her plate. "I met my first ghost in St. Mary's."

Dad frowns a little. "That's a hospital, isn't it?"

"Yes," she says briskly, "I was quite sick once. Scarlet fever."

Mom brings her hand to her mouth. "Your parents must have been so worried."

Lara looks up, blinking quickly. "Oh, yes, they were." She looks down again. "I got better, obviously, but they kept me there a while, on the ward, and one night, I couldn't sleep. Someone was *singing*. Quite loudly, in the hall. But no one else seemed to hear, or notice." She stares off into space, a faraway look in her eyes. "So I got up, and went to find them."

"And tell them off," says Jacob, teasing.

Lara's gaze cuts toward him, but she doesn't stop talking. "There was this curtain in front of the door, and when I pushed it aside, the voice was so much clearer. So I followed it. And I found her, around the corner, at the end of the hall, looking out the window and singing. She was holding a baby, and the moonlight was streaming through, one of those bright spotlight moons, and I could see straight through both of them."

I shiver a little.

But Lara only straightens, and smiles, and says, quite briskly, "Of course, afterward, I knew, it must have been a fever dream. I was still quite sick, after all. But I never forgot that woman, or the singing, or the child in her arms."

The table is quiet for a long moment.

In the end, it's Jacob, of course, who breaks the silence.

"You know, I thought the creepiest thing in the world was children singing, but I take it back. It might be that."

Lara and I both laugh, and Mom and Dad look at us as if we've lost our minds.

After dinner, we make our way back through the maze of garden and gate and start back toward the Quarter. The streets around us are filled with people, and I scan them all, holding my breath as I search for a broad-brimmed hat, a skull-faced mask. Jacob walks backward, checking behind us. Lara glances around, too, even as she carries on with Dad and Mom, talking about the histories of New Orleans neighborhoods.

But I'm still thinking about Lara's story. Did she know what to do? Even then, did she know that she'd crossed into the Veil, that the woman there was a ghost, a trapped spirit, waiting to be sent on?

She couldn't have known then, right?

And yet, it's hard to imagine a version of Lara Chowdhury that *doesn't* know.

Hard to imagine she was ever scared or confused.

"Listen," says Mom, wrapping her arms around my shoulders. "Do you hear that?"

And suddenly, I'm on edge again, fingers going to the evil eye in my pocket as I listen. I hear the constant murmurs of the Veil, the vague melody of whispers and songs, but closer, clearer, I hear what Mom does. A beat, as steady as a heart or a drum. Lara and Dad and Jacob hear it, too, their heads turning toward the sound.

"What is that?" I ask.

But Mom only flashes a dazzling smile and says, "Let's find out."

She grabs my hand, and we're off.

When I was young, Mom and I would go for walks in the fields and woods beyond our house. There was no path, no set course. If anything, she would change direction as often as she could, getting turned around on purpose. We were never far from home, but at the time, the world felt so wild and big, and I was scared of going too far, of not finding my way back.

But Mom loved it. Believed it was all part of the adventure.

She said the best way to find yourself was to let yourself get lost.

It's hard to get lost in the grid of streets, but it's easy to get turned around.

I catch Lara's hand in mine, and Jacob catches hers, and Dad is on our heels, and together, we follow the drum, and the trumpet that joins in, the brash shout of a horn, and the metallic ring of whistles.

The volume rises like a tide.

A chaotic melody, vibrant and alive.

The music swells as we round a corner, and suddenly, we're face-to-face with a parade.

Not a jazz funeral like earlier—there are no white suits, no somberness to the affair, no casket that I can see—just shining brass instruments, and brilliant costumes, and *skeletons*. I tense, instantly on guard. But the skeletons only billow like kites on bright red strings, dancing in the air, jaws open as if laughing. Lara's hand tightens around mine, but despite everything, I'm not afraid.

There is no menace in the air, no danger. No bone-deep chill or hollowing fear.

Just the overwhelming thrum of energy and life.

We stand there a moment, two parents, two girls, and a ghost, watching the parade. With every forward step, it seems to gain size. People join, cheering and dancing, the procession swelling into a street party.

"What are they celebrating?" I call over the roar of the crowd.

"Life!" says Mom. "Death!" she adds. "And everything in between."

"Can we join?" I ask, and Mom beams, as if she thought I'd never ask.

We step into the fray. The parade swirls around us, carries us along, and we let it. I want to close my eyes, disappear into the sound, but I don't want to get trampled.

"Life is a party, dear daughter," says Mom, draping a chain of gold beads around my neck. "Celebrate it every day."

Dad snags a feathered crown and sets it on Lara's head, and for an instant, she looks so surprised, so out of place, that Jacob cackles, and I expect her to take it off, to smooth her hair. But she doesn't. She smiles. And sure, she straightens the crown a little when it slips to one side, and holds it there, but only because she doesn't want to lose it while she's dancing.

And there, in the midst of the parade, she is not Lara Chowdhury, a lonely girl trying to grow up too fast. She's just Lara, smart and clever and selfless.

And Jacob Ellis Hale is not the ghost of a boy who drowned three years ago in a river, trying to rescue his little brother's toy. He's just my best friend, bouncing out of time with the beat.

And I'm not being hunted by an agent of Death.

I'm just a girl dancing with my friends and family in the street.

CHAPTER SEVENTEEN

We tumble back into our hotel room, giddy and tired.

My shoe knocks against something small and hard, and it goes skittering across the floor. A stone. I look down and see another, then the open box of matches, spilling thin wood sticks across the floor.

The room wasn't exactly tidy to start with, but now it's a *mess*.

"Oh dear," says Mom.

And for a second, I wonder if we somehow caught the attention of a poltergeist here. And then I realize, this wasn't a spirit at work.

It was a *cat*.

Grim has not only gotten into Lara's backpack, he's pulled out everything he could reach. The cat was a small black tornado of destruction, scattering all our supplies around the room.

The bottle of oil is nowhere to be seen. The ball of white string has been unraveled, and tangled through the legs of the table and around the chair. Only the pouch of grave dirt has been left mercifully closed, though the culprit sits squarely on top of it, his black tail flicking nervously from side to side.

When I try to nudge Grim off, his ears go back, and his nails dig into the pouch, as if to say *mine*. Or maybe *bad*.

I reach for the pouch again, and he bats my hand away in warning. Perhaps he's trying to protect me after all, telling me to stay away from this symbol of death.

Or maybe he's just an ornery cat.

Dad hoists Grim up and plants him on the sofa, and Lara offers up her feathered crown to the cat as a distraction while I kneel on the floor, carefully scooping up the thin gray dust that spilled through the tiny holes where Grim's claws punctured the cloth.

It takes ten minutes to find all the stones and pick up the loose matches.

"What is all this?" asks Mom, fetching the bottle of oil from where it rolled under the bed.

"Oh," says Lara quickly. "Just some gifts I bought for my parents."

"Speaking of which," says Dad, making a tidy pile of the small black stones, "your aunt must be wondering where you are."

Lara and I exchange a look.

"Actually," she says, putting on her best grown-up voice, "Cass invited me to spend the night and my aunt agreed. If that's all right with you."

I exhale a little, trying to hide my relief. "That's really nice of your aunt," I say.

"I know." Lara smiles. "She's very thoughtful."

Mom wavers. "It's fine with us," she says, "but I really would feel better if we called her to check."

I hold my breath, waiting for Lara's lie to fall apart, but she just nods and says, "Of course," before pulling out her phone. It rings and rings, and I wonder if she's called a real number at all when a voice answers.

"Hello! Hello! Thread and Bo—"

"Aunt Philly!" Lara calls in a bright, chiming voice. "It's me, Lara."

I can just make out Philippa's whimsical voice on the other end. "Well, hello again."

"Cassidy's parents want to make sure I'm safe and sound, and that you're okay with me spending the night. Will you speak to them?"

Lara hands the phone to Mom, shooting me a mischievous look. I can't help but wonder if Lara has a little bit of Slytherin mixed in with all that Ravenclaw.

That night, when Mom and Dad are asleep, and the lights are out, and Lara's backpack is safely stored in the bathroom with the door closed to protect it from the cat, she and Jacob and I make a tent under the covers of my bed, and talk.

We sit, knees close and heads together, our faces lit by the flashlight on Lara's phone.

In this jagged light, we're all washed out, and it's easy to forget that Jacob's a ghost. I can barely see through him, and I swear, if Mom and Dad were to look over now, they might see three figures in the tent instead of two.

Thankfully, they're fast asleep.

"You're breathing on me," mutters Lara, leaning away from Jacob. "It's . . . cold. I don't like it."

"What am I supposed to do?" mutters Jacob. "Hold my breath?"

"Do you even need air?" she snaps back.

"Focus," I hiss.

We'd been discussing the steps for the banishing ritual.

"So what do we do tomorrow?" Jacob asks. "We just wait for the Emissary to show back up?"

"That," I say, "or we go looking for it."

Jacob stares at me like I've lost my mind. I get it. When I think of running *toward* the Emissary, my legs feel like jelly. But the idea of getting caught off guard might be worse.

In the end, we take a vote. Jacob is solidly in the "don't go looking for Death" camp, and to my surprise, so is Lara.

"I think we should be prepared," she says. "But if we go after it, the Emissary might sense a trap."

I take a deep breath. "So we let it find me."

And take you back into the dark.

Jacob's the one who can read my mind, but Lara's the one who squeezes my hand. "We're in this together. And you're not going anywhere."

She pulls her hand away to cover a yawn, and it's contagious, bouncing from her to me to Jacob.

"We should sleep," I say, even though I don't know if I can.

We discuss taking shifts, then realize it's pointless, since Jacob is the only one who doesn't *need* sleep. Lara mumbles something about not trusting a ghost and a lazy cat to keep us safe all night, but she's too tired to do more than protest.

We collapse our makeshift tent, and Jacob goes to the foot of the bed and sits there, back to us, staring into the dark. "Night, Cass," he whispers.

"Night, Jacob," I whisper, my head on my pillow.

"Mnmnghost," whispers Lara, already half asleep next to me.

I don't know what'll happen tomorrow.

I don't know if I'll be able to banish the Emissary.

I don't know if we can win.

But right now, tucked between my family and my friends, I feel almost safe.

I lie awake, listening to the murmur of the Veil, and

the very real noise of people in the streets, and the distant sound of the party still going somewhere, faint and far away as wind. I pull the evil eye from my pajama pocket and think through the banishing spell again, turning the glass charm between my fingers until the pattern of black, blue, white, blue becomes abstract, just streaks of colored glass, until I can't keep my own eyes open any longer.

I don't remember falling asleep, but one second I'm in bed, and the next, I'm in the cemetery.

I scramble backward as the Emissary appears, making its slow, steady way toward me between the crypts. I call for Jacob, for Lara, but I have no voice. I turn and run, until I reach a dead end, a crypt that stretches as far and wide as I can see. I burst through the door and into the tomb. There's no casket, only a statue of the blindfolded girl from the Two of Swords, the blades crossed in front of her.

The girl is made of stone, but the swords are metal—heavy and real.

The door rattles and shakes behind me as I pull the swords out of the statue's hands.

I turn to face the Emissary as it bursts through the door, but I wake right before it reaches me.

My heart is racing and the room is dark, my hand aching where it grips the evil eye. But when I force my fingers open, the charm is unbroken, and Lara is asleep, and Jacob is right there, in front of the bed. He glances over his shoulder and makes a silly face. My heart slows, and I smile and sink back into the sheets.

The rest of the night is restless, dreamless, and I'm relieved when light slips through the window curtains. I get up and shower, wrangle my messy curls back and up, reach for my mirror pendant before remembering it's broken.

I comb through Mom's toiletry bag and find a compact, a disc of blush on one side and a smudged mirror on the other. It'll do for now.

One of the first things Lara taught me was that in-betweeners should never be without a mirror.

Look and listen. See and know. This is what you are.

The words reserved for a ghost.

But they hold true for the living, too.

I meet my gaze in the compact mirror's reflection. "My name is Cassidy Blake," I say softly. "I'm twelve years old. Last year, I stole from Death. I lived when I should have died. I stayed when I should have gone. I survived once, and I'll survive again. My name is Cassidy Blake," I say again. "And I will not be dragged into the dark."

PART FOUR

THE EMISSARY OF DEATH

CHAPTER EIGHTEEN

There are two ways to find Death.

Either you go looking for it, or you wait for it to come to you.

We chose the latter, but as the morning goes on, I'm beginning to regret that choice. Lara, Jacob, and I trail my parents and their film crew through haunted hotels. Apparently, it's hard to find a hotel in New Orleans *without* a resident ghost. According to Lucas, half the hotels were schools or orphanages once, until, like the Place d'Armes, all of them burned down.

Where are you? I think as we stand in a room in the Bourbon Orleans, while Mom's EMF meter warbles and whines, and once, I swear, it even *giggles*. I shiver and retreat, leaning against a wall, only to feel the Veil lean back, whispering mischief.

"Come and play."

But I resist the pull. Ghost hunting is officially on hold.

We go to more hotels: the Monteleone, the Andrew Jackson, the Dauphine. At each one, the cameras roll, and Dad recounts the history of the hotel and Mom recounts the stories of its ghosts. Of shadows that sit on the edges of beds and children who play in the halls. Of things that go missing and things that are found.

It's hard to focus on the filming. My nerves tighten, my senses bristle. I keep my ears tuned to the air, waiting for any shift. For the sound to drop out of the room, or a chill breeze, or a voice drifting through the dark.

We will find you, it said.

Come and try, I think.

I can tell that Jacob and Lara are just as jumpy, though he's no good at hiding it, and somehow she's able to smile and pretend that she's listening to my parents' show, that the only thing making her shiver is one of Mom's stories.

Lara keeps her hand on her backpack, ready to assemble the banishing spell as soon as the Emissary makes its move.

But several locations later and still no sign of it.

The sun is high and hot as we pass the Old Ursuline Convent, a massive building that looms behind tall walls and sculpted hedges.

According to Dad, the convent is older than the United States. According to Mom, it's the birthplace of the American vampire. Or at least, one of the vampire legends. Apparently, teenage girls were sent over from France, and they arrived in New Orleans pale and gaunt, clutching casket-shaped boxes. The boxes—called caskets—were supposed to contain their dowry. But the myths grew until people believed that the boxes were literal caskets, and the girls undead.

As Mom and Dad narrate, I keep one hand in my pocket, fingers tight around the glass evil eye, and wait, and wait, and wait. But I don't feel anything strange, save for the rise and fall of the Veil.

Maybe I should feel relieved. But I don't. Instead, I feel like someone who's holding her breath, and running out of air.

I knew we would end up here eventually.

The most haunted place in New Orleans.

We stand in front of the LaLaurie Mansion, looking up at the squat stone building, stretching as wide as the block.

"You know," says Jacob, "I was just starting to think, as far as ghosts go, this city isn't so bad."

I stare at the house. It's three stories tall instead of the Quarter's usual two, which makes it loom over the low buildings to either side like a shadow, despite its pale gray stone.

And I shudder, despite the heat.

I've been to Mary King's Close, where people were bricked into the walls while still alive.

I've been to the Catacombs of Paris, with its millions of bones.

Places where the past seeped through, the voices and emotions carried on the Veil.

And even from the street, I know this is one of those places. And suddenly, I think I'd rather face my own death again than go inside.

The front door sits back from the curb, crypt white beneath a stone arch, the entrance barred by a black iron gate. The tips of the bars are spiked like arrows, and it feels like the opposite of an invitation.

Go away, the building seems to say.

I look around, almost hoping for a visit from the

Emissary, but there's still no sign of it as Lucas pulls a key from his pocket and unlocks the door, a stale draft seeping out.

I remember Adan's story from the first night, about the call coming from inside the house, even though no one else was home. And I know it was the kind of ghost story you tell instead of the true horror, the kind you tell about places after they're haunted, instead of the ones that explain how they got haunted in the first place.

"There are many shadows in New Orleans's past," says Dad, "but this is one of the darkest."

His voice is low and stern, but I can tell he's speaking to the camera.

We step through the door, and the Veil *slams* into me.

A wave of hatred and pain and fear so sharp it knocks the air from my lungs. Lara sucks in a breath, and I can tell she feels it, too. The weight of ruined places. The anger of the dead. Smoke burns my eyes, even though the front hall is cold and bare, and a heavy beat sounds in my ears, like knuckles knocking on wood.

"Madame LaLaurie was a socialite," says Mom, with none of her usual cheer, "and a serial killer. At a time when the horrors of slavery ran rampant in this country, LaLaurie stands out for the sheer scope of her cruelty."

Lucas looks down at the marble floor, his hands clenched into fists.

"It came to light during one of her parties," says Dad. "A fire started, and quickly spread through the house. Everyone got out in time, or so they thought. And yet, there were voices coming from the burning house." He swallows hard. "Even after the fire was put out, they heard pleading, and the dull pounding of fists. It was only when the ashes cooled that they discovered why."

He looks down.

"LaLaurie had kept her slaves locked in the attic."

Bile rises in my throat.

"When the fire started, they had no way to escape."

Jacob shudders. Lara's hand goes to her mouth. The Veil reaches out, ready to pull me through, and I push back with all my might because I can't face the other side, and for once, it has nothing to do with the Emissary.

"Some events are so terrible," says Mom, "they seep into the bones of a place. They stain its past, its present, and its future." She gestures around her. "This is an angry house.

As it should be. Madame LaLaurie was never punished for her monstrous crime. She and her husband fled to France, leaving pain and injustice in their wake." Mom takes a deep breath, and steps, like a diver, down the darkened hall. But I'm not ready to follow.

I'm relieved when Lucas steps in front of me.

"You should go," he says quietly. "This is no place for . . ." I wonder if he's about to say in-betweeners, but after a moment he just says, "children."

Usually, I'd protest, insist I'm old enough for whatever's waiting inside, but this time, I don't want to get closer. I can't bear the thought of those rooms. I wish I didn't know what happened here, even though Mom says that knowing is a kind of respect. A way of honoring the dead.

"Are you coming?" Dad asks me and Lara.

"I don't think they should," says Lucas. My parents and our guide exchange a three-way look, the kind of silent conversation grown-ups have sometimes.

And then Dad nods and says, "You're right."

He hands me some cash and tells us to go get a snack, to meet them outside the mansion in an hour. With that, the Inspecters and their crew head deeper into the darkened house, and Jacob and Lara and I back out onto the street. The Veil retreats as we step beyond the iron gate. I lean against a lamppost, shaking from the force of it.

"When *I* say we should skip the haunted house, you never listen . . ." Jacob mutters.

We set out down Royal, eager to put as much distance between us and the LaLaurie Mansion as possible.

As we walk and walk, I can't help but wonder, *where* is the Emissary?

My nerves were wound tight before the LaLaurie Mansion, but now they've officially snapped. "This isn't working," I say. "We tried waiting. And it hasn't come."

"Maybe it gave up," says Jacob. "Maybe it's like a game of hide-and-seek, and we hid long enough, and now the game's over."

"Do you honestly believe that?" asks Lara.

Jacob frowns. "It could be true."

But we all know it's not.

And we all know what we have to do. We have to get Death's attention.

Jacob, of course, thinks it's a bad idea.

"No," he says, "I think it's a *really* bad idea. Like, a

monumentally bad idea. First, it's dangerous. Second, it's full of things that could go wrong. And third, I hate it." He sighs. "But if this is what we have to do, let's do it. Um . . . how do we do it?"

We stop at the corner, and I look up and down the streets. They're crowded with cars and carriages and people. Jazz fills the air, along with laughter and horns. The Quarter is busy today.

"It's here somewhere," I say. "It has to be. So why isn't it showing up?"

"It's too crowded," says Lara, gesturing at the street. "The girl with the Rubik's Cube yesterday, Hazel? She said that New Orleans was a good place to hide, because it's so *busy*. And we've spent all day in crowded places. So if we don't *want* to hide, we need to find somewhere quiet."

I nod. "So that we stand out. Like I did in the graveyard."

We discuss going to St. Louis or Lafayette, but it's a Sunday, and the weather is cooler, which means the cemeteries will be packed with tourists.

"What about a séance?" asks Jacob.

Lara rolls her eyes. "I told you those aren't real," she says, and she's right. But so is Jacob. After all, we had a séance, and the Emissary came. Sure, it was only a voice, but it found me there.

I don't think we need all the bells and whistles of a séance. Maybe we just need to use the room in the Hotel Kardec.

My spirits lift, until Jacob reminds me it's locked up. Off-limits.

I groan, running my hands through my hair as we start walking again.

Think, think.

The Veil rises and falls around me, carrying smoke and jazz, and the whispers I've come to recognize as Jackson Square. I slam to a stop. Turn left. And there it is, on the edge of the square.

Muriel's.

Muriel's, with its ivy-strewn restaurant, and its large stairs, and the weird, antique-filled room up top.

The *séance* room.

I glance at Lara and Jacob. "Follow me."

CHAPTER NINETEEN

The downstairs restaurant is packed for lunch. We head straight for the staircase, but a waiter stops us.

"Are you kids lost?" he asks.

Lara bristles visibly at being called a *kid*, but I just shake my head.

"We have a date with Death," says Jacob, but thankfully the waiter can't hear him.

"School project," I say, holding up my camera.

The waiter eyes us with suspicion, but then someone somewhere drops a tray, and he waves us on and says, "Just don't touch anything."

"Of course not," says Lara, in her best, brightest British.

As we climb the staircase, a couple comes down the other way, arm in arm, drinking and chatting about how *spooky* it is up there, what wonderful *ambience*. We pass them, and Lara looks back over her shoulder.

"Is this part open to the public?" she asks me.

I nod, and she looks around, then grabs an EMPLOYEES ONLY sign on a chain and hangs it across the top of the stairs behind us.

"This way," I say, leading her past the cushioned lounge, into the red light of the séance room, with its eerie dark-room glow.

"Well, this is charming," says Lara, scanning the old paintings and the grinning masks, the strange combination of statues and animal prints and fancy furniture.

"Ten out of ten for atmosphere," agrees Jacob.

A quick survey, and I'm satisfied that no one else is up here with us. For right now, at least, we have the séance room to ourselves.

"Ready?" asks Lara, and the question feels so much bigger than it is, but I nod.

"Let's do this."

We dump the supplies out of Lara's red backpack, matches and oil and grave dirt tumbling out onto an otto-man. There's an ornate silk rug on the floor, and I pull it aside, exposing the bare wood floors beneath, mottled with age.

The last thing we need is to start a fire.

"I thought that was exactly what we're doing," says Jacob.

"You know what I mean," I say. "A bigger fire."

The kind that gets out of control.

Lara opens the pouch of grave dirt and tips some out into her palm. It looks more like sand than soil, dry and gray, but there's a faint odor, not like something rotting, exactly, just like something *gone*. The lifeless smell of old, abandoned places.

She traces out a circle with the small black stones, roughly the size of a séance table, then begins to pour the grave dirt out onto the floor, not in a pile but in a thin line, the way Magnolia told us to when we were in the Veil.

"I have to admit," Lara says, dusting off her palms, "I've never done anything like this before."

She hands me the bottle of oil, and I tug the stopper out.

"Which part?" I say as the room fills with the scent of sage. "Co-opting a séance room, preparing a ritual ceremony, or banishing an agent of Death?"

"All of it. It's rather exhilarating," she says, and then, seeing my face, she quickly adds, "if you don't think too hard about why we're doing it."

Lara draws a groove in the grave dirt, a narrow channel that goes all the way around the circle, and I pour the oil in, careful to save enough that it will reach, from start to end. When it's lit, the oil will burn through the grave dirt, creating a line of fire and ash, life and death, and when it does, it should cut the line between the Emissary and me.

As long as the Emissary is standing inside the circle.

Now all we have to do is lure it here, and get it to pass within the circle, and light the oil, and burn the space between us clean.

Oh no. This *is* a terrible idea.

It will never work.

It will never—

"It will," says Jacob firmly. "It has to."

He heads out into the lounge to be our lookout, for both humans and Emissaries, and after that, there's nothing to do but wait.

So we wait.

Lara wanders the room, admiring the strange and morbid decorations. I perch on the edge of a velvet sofa, get up, switch to a chair, get up again, unable to sit still. Silence settles over us like a sheet, and my ears adjust, not only to the Veil, but to the sounds in the living world.

The tinny old-fashioned music that drifts through the room.

The guests outside, murmuring as they reach the EMPLOYEES ONLY sign, saying that they thought it was open before drifting back downstairs.

The faint groan of the floorboards as Jacob rocks back and forth on his heels beyond the door.

"'Because I could not stop for Death,'" says Lara under her breath, "'He kindly stopped for me. The Carriage held but just Ourselves, and Immortality.'"

I stare at her for a long moment.

"Emily Dickinson," she says, as if that explains everything.

She goes quiet after that, and we wait for what feels like an hour, but, according to a clock on the wall, is only about ten minutes.

Jacob drifts back into the room. "Nothing," he says, looking nervous. "What now?"

My heart sinks. All of this, for nothing. We can't get

oil back into the bottle. We can't get the grave dirt back into the bag. We have to go through with this. We have to get the Emissary here. Now.

I get to my feet.

"Where are you going?" asks Lara.

"Into the Veil." Jacob and Lara both look horrified, so I explain. "We need to get the Emissary's attention, right? Well, Renée said the light in my chest was a beacon. That if I go into the Veil, I'll stand out, and it will be easier for the Emissary to find me."

"Right," says Lara.

"So . . . if you want to catch a fish . . ."

Lara nods. "You need bait."

"I don't like this," says Jacob.

"Do you have a better idea?"

"Of course not!" he says, and then groans. "Come on, let's do it."

"Be careful," says Lara.

"Be ready," I answer.

I fling aside the curtain, brace myself against the drop, the instant of cold, and then I'm back, in the séance room, the same, and not the same. I look down, and see the echo of the circle we've made on the floor, a shadow of it, as if it's burned through one world into the other.

And I think, this might actually work.

I take a deep breath, and shout as loud as I can.

"I'M NOT AFRAID OF YOU!"

The Veil swallows up my words, smothering them, but I don't care.

"COME AND GET ME!" I call, screaming out my anger and my fear. I shout until my lungs start to ache, and my head starts to swim, and Jacob takes my hand.

"I think you made your point," he says, pulling me back through the Veil.

A shudder, a gasp, and the red-lit séance room comes into focus. I steady myself as Lara looks up from the floor and shakes her head.

Nothing.

We hold our breath and wait, but the seconds tick by, and no one comes.

Lara holds out the unbroken evil eye charm. "I don't think it's working."

"This doesn't make sense!" I snap, right before I hear the sound.

The same sound my mirror made back in the graveyard, when the Emissary flung it against the tomb. The quiet crack of glass.

Lara and I both look down. The evil eye lies splintered in her palm.

And we both know what that means.

It's coming.

"Are you sure?" asks Jacob. "There's no sign of . . ." He trails off. Or really, his voice fades out, along with all the other sounds in the room. The tinny music drops away. The world goes silent.

The temperature falls.

I tie the white string around my wrist, and Lara takes the other end, a tether between us, an anchor.

I grip my camera, just so I can hold on to something, keep my hands from shaking and my nerve from failing as the Emissary appears.

It doesn't walk through the door.

Instead, it comes together like a storm. Slides like smoke between the pictures on the wall, through the cracks and gaps in the room. Gathers itself into a shadow, a shape: skeletal limbs in a pitch-black suit. A broad-brimmed hat and long, gloved fingers and bottomless black eyes behind a skull mask.

"*We have found you, Cassidy Blake,*" it says in that tangled rasp.

No, I think, *I've found you.*

But the Emissary isn't standing in the circle yet.

I need to make it step forward. I need to step back.

But my legs are locking up again. It's the skull mask, or rather, the thing behind it. That darkness that reaches out and pins me still.

The Emissary holds out its hand, as if I'd simply take it. As if, after fighting *so* hard to stay alive, I'd give up that easily.

And yet, I feel my fingers twitch.

My hand drifting up.

I can't get away. I can't *look* away.

"Cassidy!"

Jacob's voice cuts through like a flash.

A flash. My camera.

I force the camera up and look through the viewfinder, use the lens instead of my own eyes, and instantly my head clears. My legs come unstuck from the floor.

"Come and get me," I snap, trying to keep my voice from shaking as I step back out of reach. And the Emissary steps forward, over the line of the circle.

"Lara! Now!"

She strikes a match. It doesn't light.

She strikes a second. It flares, and then goes out.

"Lara!" I say, panic winding through my voice as the Emissary takes another step forward. It's standing in the middle of the circle now, but soon, it will be at the front, and then it will be out, and—

The third match strikes. And lights.

Lara brings it to the oil, and the circle begins to burn.

The Emissary stops.

Looks down, its mask tilting to one side, clearly confused.

I thought it would go up fast, a struck match, a sudden burst of flame. The circle lit, and closed, in an instant. Instead, the fire moves slowly. It pours itself in a narrow band around the Emissary's feet.

But it's working. The Emissary twitches, caught in the trap, and the flame slides around the circle, closing the loop and—

"Cassidy," says Jacob, his voice unsteady. I turn toward

him. I know Jacob—from his blond curls to his superhero shirt, his bright eyes and his playful grin. But right now, he looks *wrong*. He's soaking wet, his clothes clinging to his narrow frame. He looks thin and gray, his hair floating around his face, as if he's underwater.

He says my name again, the word threaded with sadness and fear. "Cass?"

And I don't understand, until I do.

The circle.

The circle is designed to sever the line, to break the connection between the Emissary and me. But we're not the only ones tied together.

It's cutting away Jacob, too.

I'm the only thing holding him here.

And the line is breaking.

The oil continues to burn. The fire carves its thin bright way around the circle, and Jacob collapses to his hands and knees, the life going out of him.

"No!" I shout, moving toward him.

"Just a little longer!" calls Lara as the circle burns and the Emissary tries, and fails, to drag itself forward. Its edges begin to smudge, the rim of its hat dissolving into smoke. But Jacob is fading, too.

"Cassidy, don't!" warns Lara.

But I drop to his side, pleading with him to hold on, to stay. He shudders and rolls over, coughing river water onto the bare wood floor. But he's stopped thinning, stopped fading.

"I'm okay," he says, gasping for breath. "I'm okay."

But he shouldn't be. The spell's still going. And then I look down and see that my shoe has crossed the line of the circle, breaking the flame.

"Cassidy, look out!" screams Lara.

I look up, and there's the Emissary, freed from the ring and reaching straight for me. Its gloved fingers brush my skin, like an icy breeze.

And then Lara is there, throwing herself between the Emissary and me.

And the last thing I see is that gloved hand closing over her arm, before the ring of fire dies, and the grave dirt circle blows apart, and the Emissary is gone.

And so is Lara.

CHAPTER TWENTY

I sit, reeling, on the wooden floor.

In front of me, the smudged remains of the circle are still smoking.

It happened so fast. The white string is still looped around my wrist, but the other end drifts loose, abandoned. Lara's red backpack sags against the sofa, the only sign she was here.

This isn't right.

The Emissary was only after *me*.

But the truth settles like a weight on my chest. Emissaries are drawn to in-betweeners. To all those who've cheated death. Which means even though it came for me, Lara was always in danger, too.

"Cass," says Jacob, still shaking off the spell.

But I'm already on my feet. I have to find Lara. She can't have gone that far.

I scramble up, grabbing her backpack, as I reach for the

223

Veil. I swing the bag over my shoulder, catch hold of the curtain, and throw it aside, trading one séance room for another. The smoldering ruins of our banishing circle scar the floor, but otherwise, there's no sign of Lara, or the Emissary.

I run down the stairs, through the burning–not burning house and out into the crowded square. My vision doubles again from the overlapping Veils, and everywhere I look, I see ghosts and phantoms, carriages and fires and parades.

But there's no sign of Lara.

I close my eyes and try to feel the pull of her thread, the thing all in-betweeners share, but the Veil is so messy, so chaotic, I can't think over the noise, can't feel anything but panic, so I shout her name.

I shout until it draws the attention of the spirits. Until a handful of ghosts start drifting toward me.

"Cass," says Jacob, at my side. "She's not here."

But she has to be.

She can't . . .

Tears prick my eyes, blurring my vision until the square is nothing but vague shapes and shades of gray, a world out of focus.

Focus.

My camera. Every time I looked at the Emissary through the lens, it was an inky mass, a pitch-black pool against the backdrop of the world. I lift the camera now, and look through it, sliding the focus on the lens as I scan the crowded square, looking for the darkness, the shadow on the frame, searching for something, anything out of place.

Nothing, nothing—and then I see it.

A horseless carriage.

It's black as night, black as the space behind the skull's eyes, and it's cutting straight through the crowd, surging away and out of the square.

And I *know* Lara's in there.

She's not gone, not yet.

But I have to find out where she's going.

I start forward after the carriage, colliding with a ghost.

He scowls and shoves me. "Watch it, girl."

I lower my camera, and the square comes back into violent focus, a teeming mass of movement and spirits, too many starting toward me.

Jacob pulls me away from the ghosts, even as I lift the

camera and slide the focus, still searching, searching. But I've lost sight of the carriage.

We cut back into the world of the living, the transition so jarring I have to brace myself against the wall for a moment until my vision clears. My heart races in my chest, with panic, but also with hope.

The horseless carriage must be going somewhere.

I just don't know where.

I don't know how long I have.

I don't know, I don't know, I don't know.

But I know people who will.

I take off, down one block and up another, skidding to a stop in front of Thread & Bone. I fling open the door. Or I try to, but it holds fast. I push again before noticing that the sign on the glass says CLOSED.

No, no, no.

I rattle the handle. I pound on the door. But the lights are off, and no one answers, and I can't get through to the Society room and all the old members without being let in *by* a Society member.

Jacob peers through the glass, then pulls back, shaking his head. "No one's here," he says. "Except the cat."

This can't be happening. Not now.

I *need* the Society.

"Cassidy," he says, "we know where one of them is."

Of course. Lucas Dumont.

Official Inspecters guide. And Society historian.

I'm breathless and queasy by the time we get back to the LaLaurie Mansion, the heat smothering my lungs. I'm secretly hoping that my parents and the crew will all be standing on the curb waiting for us, but it hasn't been an hour yet, and they're not outside, and I don't have time. *Lara* doesn't have time.

I push open the gate, step back into the arched alcove, and the Veil rises in warning. I step through the door, into the darkened foyer, and the other side groans and pushes at me, but there's no sign of my parents, or the film crew, or Lucas.

I listen, trying to make out their voices over the pounding in my head, and hear footsteps overhead. I hurry down the hall, but the moment my foot hits the stairs, the Veil surges around me, carrying the clink of champagne glasses and the wave of an anguished scream, as high and long as a kettle whistling on the stove. Waves of anger and grief fold over me as the Veil forces me to my hands and knees on the steps.

No, no, no, I think as it reaches up through the floor, the thin gray curtain wrapping tight around my wrists as it pulls me down.

Jacob pulls me back.

The airy pressure of his hands on my shoulders: the only thing holding me here in the land of the living.

"Don't let go," I plead, throwing all my energy against the other side.

He shimmers a little with the effort. "I've got you," he says, holding as tight as a ghost can as I look up and see Mom and Dad coming down the stairs.

"Cassidy?" says Mom.

I don't know what they've felt or seen in here, but the EMF meter is shut off in Mom's hand, and Dad's mouth is set in a grim line. Lucas trails behind them, along with Jenna and Adan, their cameras hanging at their sides, their faces drawn. Lucas looks at me, brow furrowing when he sees I'm alone, but Dad's the one who asks.

"Where's Lara?"

I swallow, struggling to form the lie. "She's . . . with her aunt."

The words are weak, my voice cracking.

"Are you okay?" asks Mom, and the question makes my eyes burn. I can't bring myself to say yes, so I shake my head and say, "I don't feel well. Can I go back to the hotel?"

Dad presses the back of his hand against my forehead, and Mom looks worried. It's only been a few days since I fainted in Paris.

"Of course," says Dad.

Only Lucas seems to sense that something went wrong, though I don't know if it's the lie, or the pleading in my eyes when I look at him.

"I'll walk Cass back to the hotel," says Lucas.

"Are you sure?" asks Mom. "We have the B-roll to film but—"

"It's no trouble at all," he says, and I gratefully follow him out the door, Jacob on our heels.

"What happened?" Lucas asks as soon as we're outside, and it spills out of me: our idea to lure the Emissary, the setup in the séance room, how everything went right until the moment it went wrong, how the Emissary took Lara instead of me, the horseless carriage I saw in the square, the Society headquarters closed.

"I have a key," says Lucas, pulling it out from his pocket as we hurry toward the shop.

"I don't know where it's taking her," I ramble. "She wasn't in danger until I—"

"She was always in danger, Cassidy," Lucas says. "She understood that, even if you didn't."

Tears spill down my face, and I dash them away. She's not gone. Lara Chowdhury is the smartest, most stubborn girl I know. She's not gone.

I just have to find her.

I can't read Jacob's mind the way he reads mine, but I can tell he feels guilty, too. We couldn't have known the spell would hurt him.

The tarot card reading whispers in my head.

No matter what you choose, you will lose.

"You should have let me go," Jacob whispers now, and if he were flesh and bone, I would punch him.

Instead, I snap, "Well, I didn't. I couldn't. I won't. I'm not losing either of my friends today."

Lucas looks at me, but doesn't seem flustered by the fact I'm yelling at someone he can't see. I wonder if he's *ever* been flustered. He reminds me of Lara in that way. If Lara were here instead of me, she would know what to do. I try to summon her voice in my head. *Slow down*, it would say. *Stay calm, just think*.

I take a deep breath. "One of the past members of the Society said that if the Emissary caught me, it would take me back, to the place *beyond* the Veil."

Lucas nods, pushing his glasses up his face. "That makes sense. According to most of the accounts I've read, the world is broken into three spaces. The land of the living, the Veil between, and the place beyond."

"I know how to get from the living to the Veil," I say. "There's a kind of *curtain*. But how do you get from the Veil to the place beyond?"

"I'm not an in-betweener," says Lucas, shaking his head as we cross a busy street. "But I've read enough to know it's called the Bridge of Souls. It sits at the far edge of the Veil. The good news is, it isn't a curtain, or a door. It's a place that must be crossed. Sometimes it's a road, sometimes it's a tower filled with stairs, sometimes—"

"Could it be a real bridge?" asks Jacob.

"What?" I turn, and realize that Jacob has stopped walking. He's standing in front of a tourist shop, staring at a large map of the city in the window. And he's pointing at something. I double back and stand beside him, surveying the map. There's the French Quarter and the Garden District, the cemeteries scattered like graves across the city.

I follow Jacob's hand up, to the top left edge of the frame, where the crescent of the city gives way to the coast of a massive lake.

And there, jutting out across it, is a bridge.

A bridge so long it vanishes off the side of the map.

"The Causeway," says Lucas, stepping up beside me.

And just like that, the pieces slot together in my head.

Dad's voice, when we first got here.

It's home to the longest bridge in the US. The Lake Pontchartrain Causeway—you can't see one side from the other.

The weird push-pull Jacob and I both felt in Metairie Cemetery, coming from the direction of the lake. But what if it wasn't the lake?

What if it was the *bridge*?

"Are you sure?" asks Jacob.

And the truth is, I'm not. And I know that if I'm wrong, I could be too late; I could lose Lara.

But if Lara were here, she would tell me that I'm an in-betweener, and I have to learn to trust my gut. And if I close my eyes, and manage to quiet the sounds of the Quarter, the chaotic rhythm of the Veil, I can feel *something*. The opposite of the force that draws me toward Lara. That push instead of a pull, like magnets facing the wrong way.

I point in the direction of the feeling and open my eyes.

"Is the bridge that way?" I ask.

And Lucas nods.

"Spirit compass," says Jacob. "It's like a brand-new superpower."

Which is great, but we're in the middle of the French Quarter, and judging by the map, the bridge is miles away.

"How do we get there?" I ask, but Lucas already has his phone out.

"I know someone who can help," he says, making a call.

I can hear a bubbly voice answer on the other end. "Hello, hello!"

"Hi, Philippa," he says. "We've got an emergency. Code Seven. Can you bring the car? Yes, to Thread and Bone."

"Code Seven?" I ask when he hangs up. "What does that stand for?"

"Don't ask questions," says Lucas.

I flinch. "Sorry, I was just wondering—"

"No," says Lucas, "Code Seven means don't ask questions. We had to add it, because Philippa's rather chatty, and sometimes, time is of the essence."

We stand on the curb and wait, my chest tightening with every passing moment as I shift Lara's red backpack on my shoulder and clutch the broken evil eye in my pocket as if it will buy me time.

Hang on, Lara, I think. *Hang on.*

"She's really smart," says Jacob. I look up at him. I'm pretty sure, when it comes to Lara, it's the first nice thing he's ever said. "She's really smart," he says again, "and stubborn, and she knows lots of tricks, so I'm sure she'll be okay until we get there."

I bite my lip and nod, hoping he's right.

"You should know," says Lucas, "Philippa's car is a bit unconventional."

I half expect to see her pull up in a horse-drawn carriage.

Instead, she arrives in something *so* much worse.

"Oh no," says Jacob as the car drives up onto the curb, looking like a stretched-out station wagon.

It's not a station wagon, of course.

It's a *hearse*.

Philippa leans out the driver's side window, her white-blond hair rising like a plume over her head, a funeral lily tucked behind one ear.

"Hello again," she says. "Someone need a ride?"

CHAPTER TWENTY-ONE

Philippa may be driving a hearse, but she treats it like a race car, running all the yellow lights and half the red ones.

"Better than an ambulance," she says brightly. "People always get out of the way."

"Careful," says Lucas as she swerves between cars, accelerates fast enough that the coffin in the back jostles and slides.

"The living are so squeamish when it comes to the dead," Philippa says.

"Sometimes the dead are squeamish, too," says Jacob, who's sitting beside me in the back. "I, for one, am not thrilled that there is a body in this car."

Well, there is a *coffin* behind us, covered in flowers. Neither of us have actually looked inside the coffin to find out if—

"Oh, that's Fred," says Philippa, waving her hand.

A shiver runs down my spine, and Jacob and I both lean forward to get farther away from the polished wood.

"So," I say, trying not to think about Fred. "You drive a hearse?"

"Not usually. I mean, it's my boyfriend's car, but he lets me borrow it when it's free."

I look over my shoulder, wondering at her definition of *free*. "Is there always a coffin in the back?"

"I told you," she says, waving her hand again. "That's just Fred."

"She's talking about the coffin," explains Lucas.

"Right, the coffin. We call him Fred," says Philippa. "He's empty," she adds, almost as an afterthought.

I sigh a little with relief, but then inhale sharply as Philippa swerves between two trucks and hits the gas. Lucas closes his eyes. And this, I think, is how I'm going to die. Again. Not in a river, and not at the Emissary's hands, but in a hearse, hurtling through afternoon traffic toward Lake Pontchartrain.

I grip the broken evil eye charm in my pocket, squeezing until my fingers ache. I wasn't sure if we were right about the bridge, but as the hearse races north, I can *feel* it, like a shadow at the edge of my sight, a patch of cold on a warm day, and I know we're going the right way.

"Music?" asks Philippa, already switching on the radio. I don't know what I expected—rock, or pop, even classical—but what spills out is a series of low gongs, a meditation track so at odds with the racing hearse and my rising panic I almost laugh.

As we drive on, I hold the red backpack in my lap, running my thumb over the stitched letter *L* I never noticed on the front.

"Do you think we'll get there in time?" I ask.

I probably just want an adult to lie and tell me things are going to be okay, but Lucas says nothing, and Philippa looks at me in the rearview mirror and says, "I don't know, Cassidy."

And before I can get upset, she slams on the brakes, and if Jacob were corporeal, I'm pretty sure he would have gone through the front window. Instead, he braces himself against the back of the seat. I think of the display case shattering under his fist, of how strong he's getting, how, until yesterday, my biggest fear was him becoming an out-of-control spirit I'd have to send on. Everything changes so fast.

"You're staring," he says, and I blink, too quick, the way Dad does when there's a sappy commercial on and he's trying not to cry.

"Because you look funny," I say.

And he sticks out his tongue.

And I stick out mine, too.

I'm glad Jacob's not a normal ghost.

I'm glad he's stronger than ever.

I need him to be.

I don't want to lose him.

I don't want to lose Lara.

I don't want to lose anyone.

There is no victory without defeat, said the fortune-teller, but *Dad* said you can't tell the future, because we haven't lived it yet. He said that the cards were only mirrors, reflecting our own thoughts, and hopes, and fears.

So I know what I'm scared of, but I also know it isn't set in stone.

I know that I can save one of my friends without losing the other.

And I know there's a third life at stake: my own.

"We're here," says Lucas, and I look up to see the lake spreading on the horizon, a vast gray slick, as far as I can see. And cutting across it, the bridge. Philippa pulls the hearse over onto the shoulder, near the mouth of the lake. Cars go by, slowing at the sight of a stalled hearse with its flower-draped coffin in the back, but she waves them on as we all climb out.

I turn my attention to the Causeway Bridge. It stretches like taffy, a rippling line that goes straight to the horizon.

"Ready?" I ask Jacob.

"Nope," he says, but we both take a step forward. This close, I can feel the Veil, *and* the place beyond it. The Bridge of Souls. Like a pocket of silence, heavy and still.

Even in the muggy heat, it makes me shiver.

Up close, the strange push-pull is stronger. Here, it feels like repulsion. Something deep inside me warns me this is a bad place, urges me to run away.

But I can't.

I'm about to reach for the Veil when Philippa says, "Wait."

She digs in her pocket and pulls out a piece of candy, a

crumpled receipt, a fortune cookie, and a strand of braided red thread.

She plucks the red thread from the pile of odds and ends, shoves the rest in her pocket.

"Hold out your hand, Cass."

I do, expecting her to put the red thread in my palm, but instead, she wraps it several times around my wrist.

"It's easy to get lost in the space between worlds," she says. "It's like dreaming. Sometimes you forget what is and isn't real." She ties the ends into a knot. "This should help you remember."

I think of Neville Longbottom and his Remembrall, the way it turned red whenever he forgot something. The trouble, of course, was he could never remember what it was he forgot.

But all I say is "Thanks."

Philippa waves, and Lucas nods at me. "Be careful," he says.

I take a deep breath, and reach for the Veil.

The gray curtain rushes up to meet my hand. It slides between my fingers, and I catch hold, flinging it aside. I feel the lurch as the ground drops away, taking the light and color and the sound of cars with it. There's a moment of falling, of cold, and then I'm back on my feet, and the world is darker, quieter.

But here, at least, there are no dizzying layers, no double vision. Just a bleak stretch of gray.

Jacob stands beside me, his edges solid against the pale landscape.

He stares ahead. I follow his gaze, and see the bridge.

In the land of the living, it was gray, concrete, mundane. But here, it's something else. Bigger, stranger, a stretch of polished black stone that reaches as far as I can see, the end disappearing into fog. There's no water, no railing, just a long drop into shadow.

"Not ominous at all," says Jacob, aiming for his usual sarcasm and falling short. I can hear the caution in his voice, the current of fear. This is not a place either of us wants to be. Not a bridge we want to cross.

Something moves behind us, with a shudder and a sigh, and I spin. The horseless carriage is there, but it's empty. And I know Lara is out there somewhere, on the bridge.

And we have to get her back.

Once, I stole from Death.

I'm ready to do it again.

Jacob takes my hand. I squeeze, and he squeezes back, and for once, neither of us has to say a thing. Because we know. We're not alone.

Together, we step forward.

Together, we cross the line.

Together—but then a vicious gust of wind tears through, so strong I have to squeeze my eyes shut and duck my head against the whipping air. The wind pulls at my clothes and scrapes my skin, knocks the camera against my chest.

And then it's gone.

And so is Jacob.

My hand is empty, and I'm alone on the bridge. I spin, looking for him, suck in a breath to call his name, but I never get the chance.

The bridge cracks beneath my feet.

And splits.

And suddenly, I fall.

PART FIVE

THE BRIDGE OF SOULS

CHAPTER TWENTY-TWO

I'm racing against the sun.

The camera is a weight around my neck, swinging on its purple strap. (Not a candy-grape purple, but violet. My favorite color.) I've already loaded the film. I just have to get to the spot in time to take the picture.

I pedal faster, my breath coming out in plumes. That's the thing about being born along the seam between winter and spring. The sun may be warm, but the air is still cold, everything stuck between frost and melt. My tires slide a little on the pavement, but I'm a good rider, and I weave between the slick patches of black ice that linger in the shade.

The bridge comes into sight.

The sun is sliding down the sky. I know if I stop at the center of the bridge, I can catch the sun as it sinks, right there between the hills. A perfect shot. My bike tires hit the bridge, sliding from pavement to steel with a clunk, and a bad feeling hits me like a cold breeze.

But there's no time to think about it, because a truck whips around the corner and onto the bridge. I swerve out of the way, right up close to the rail, but there's room, I'm safe, I just have to keep the bike straight and—

The camera strap catches on the rail and I lurch sideways.

Everything happens so fast.

One second I'm going forward, and the next, I'm going *over*. The grind of metal on metal, bike scraping rail, the lurch of gravity, the tumble, and then the terrifying fall, nothing but empty air as the river rushes toward me.

I throw my arms up, hit the surface with all the grace of a baseball through a windowpane. Shattering.

And I remember.

I remember, I've been here before, I'm not—

But then the cold closes over me, and I can't think, can't breathe. I'm so freaked out that I actually try, and icy water rushes down my throat, choking cold. It steals up my arms and legs, drags me down.

I know how to swim, I know, but in that moment, I'm sinking. Drowning.

The surface ripples overhead, glinting, and I claw toward it, eyes blurring with icy tears. But I can't seem to go up. No matter how hard I kick, the surface doesn't get closer.

I scramble.

I panic.

I reach—

And that's when I see it.

A red lanyard wrapped around my wrist.

And I remember.

I was on the bridge. Not the one where my bike crashed. The one beyond the Veil. The Bridge of Souls. Which means this isn't happening. It's *already* happened. I crashed my bike on my birthday last year. I almost drowned. But I didn't. Because Jacob saved my life.

Jacob. We were standing together, on the Bridge of Souls. And then he was gone, and I was falling, and I was—

No, focus. Jacob. Jacob Ellis Hale, best friend and resident ghost, who died trying to rescue his little brother's favorite toy, who dove into the river and never came out.

This river.

I twist around in the dark water, looking down instead of up, and there he is. Jacob. His cheeks puffed full of air as he dives down, searches the bottom of the river, fingers closing around the figurine.

There he is, my best friend. Before he was mine, before he was—

Oh no.

This river isn't just where I *almost* died. It's where Jacob *did*.

As if on cue, the current picks up, water pulling at me, churning the silt and pebbles. Jacob tries to push off the bottom of the river, but his shoe is stuck, snagged on something he can't see.

I call out to him, or I try, but it's nothing but bubbles, air I can't afford to lose. My lungs are screaming now as Jacob crouches to free his leg and doesn't see the driftwood skimming toward his head until it's too late.

I see the driftwood hit him. I watch him fold, and then I'm swimming down, against the cold, against the current, against the drag of my own limbs.

And it's so much farther than it should be, and it's so much harder than it should be, but I reach him. He floats there, like a dreamer, as I grapple with the sticks and stones around his shoe, find the one that snagged his laces, gripped his heel.

I get him free.

By now my vision is blinking out, darkness creeping in around the edges, but all I need to do is look up, swim up, hold on to my best friend as we rise to the surface.

I break through the icy water, gasping, and Jacob sputters beside me.

"Cass?" he gasps, blinking away the darkness, the dream. "What . . . I don't . . . I was down there . . . and . . ."

"I've got you," I say as we swim toward the riverbank. But the moment we climb out of the water and onto dry ground, the muddy earth vanishes beneath my fingers, replaced by smooth stone.

We're back on the cold, dark bridge. The Bridge of Souls. Together, not quite alive, but out of that other river, and wherever it led.

Mist swirls around us, swallowing both ends of the bridge. My clothes are dry, but I'm still shivering as we get to our feet.

"We have to get out of here," says Jacob.

"Not without Lara," I snap, and he frowns at me and says, "Obviously. But how do we find her?"

I look around, but all I see is mist.

I grip Lara's red backpack on my shoulder, and close my eyes, and breathe, and try to feel the thread that binds us together, the connection that runs between all in-betweeners. But right now, I can't feel anything but the bridge. I open my eyes and squint, trying to figure out which way is back and which is forward. They both look the same, but one way feels like danger, and the other feels like home.

And that's how I know which way to go.

I go against the current of my fear.

I go *against* the urge to flee.

Against the desire to live.

And toward the far side of the bridge.

At least I'm not alone. Jacob is with me, every step. But soon, I start to feel . . . tired. The cold I felt back in the river is still winding through my bones. My teeth begin to chatter. My legs start to ache. My head is swimming, the way it does when I stay in the Veil too long.

I want to lie down.

I want to close my eyes.

I stumble, but Jacob steadies me.

"Hey, Cass," he says. "What's the fifth rule of friendship?"

"Um," I say, trying to focus. "Don't let your friends get stolen by ghosts."

"What about rule number eight?"

I exhale a cloud of pale white fog. "Don't let your friend get hit by a car."

"And number sixteen?"

I swallow, my voice getting stronger. "Don't go somewhere I can't follow."

My head is starting to clear. And up ahead, the mist thins, just enough for me to see a girl with two dark braids in a pale gray shirt, a reddish light shining through her chest.

"Lara!" I call out, but my voice does the opposite of echoing. It drops away, inches from my face, swallowed up by the heavy quiet of this place.

Up ahead, Lara sways on her feet, stumbles, and falls.

"Lara," I call as she pushes herself up and keeps walking.

"Lara!" I shout again, forcing myself forward. But she still can't hear me. When I get close, I see her eyes are open, but glassy, unfocused, as if she's in a dream.

"Lara, it's me," I say, but she doesn't blink, doesn't stop walking. "You have to wake up."

"Um, Cass," says Jacob, and I can tell by his voice that something else is wrong. I look at him, but he's looking ahead, to the place where the mist swallows the bridge.

The space there is getting darker, the gray dissolving into black.

We're almost to the end of the bridge. But Lara's still walking, the red glow flickering inside her chest.

"Lara, *stop*," I say, grabbing her arm.

But the moment my hand touches her skin, the world dissolves, the mist recoils, and all of a sudden I'm not on the bridge. I'm in a hospital room, surrounded by the slow beep of machines, the chemical-clean scent of sick places.

And there, lying in the middle of the narrow bed, is Lara.

She must be eight or nine, but she looks so small. Her tan skin is slick with sweat, her black hair matted to her face. Her breath comes out uneven, in little hitches and stutters, as if something is trapped inside her chest.

I open my mouth to say her name, but someone else says it instead.

"Lara."

I look up.

A man and woman stand on the other side of the bed, holding on to each other, their faces hollow with fear. I've never met them, but they must be Lara's parents. I see her written on their faces, her sharp eyes, her pointed chin.

A doctor stands at the foot of the bed, looking down at his sheet.

"We're doing all we can," he says. "Her heart is weak. Her fever isn't breaking . . ."

Across the bed, the man and woman look so *lost*.

"Come outside," says the doctor. "We need to talk."

And in the bed, Lara's eyelids flutter. Her mouth opens and closes, and she says, in little more than a whisper, "Please don't go."

But they don't hear her.

The doctor leads her parents out into the hall. And Lara rolls over in her fevered sleep.

I can feel the heat wafting off her skin. A reddish glow in the air, just like the light inside her chest.

And I realize: This is *her* river.

This is the moment she almost died.

And that's why we're here. That's what the Bridge of

Souls is for. That's what the Emissary wants. To change our fates. To set things right.

But this didn't happen.

I didn't drown, and Lara *won't* burn out like a light. I won't let her.

"Lara." I reach out and take her hand. It's hot, but I don't let go. I squeeze. "Wake up."

She murmurs in her sleep. "Why?"

"Because this isn't real," I say. "It's just a dream."

"Bad dream," she whispers. She sounds far away. The pulse on the hospital monitor is too slow. Her breathing is too shallow. My hand is burning up in hers, but I don't let go.

"You *have* to wake up," I say.

"I'm so tired," she murmurs.

I get it. I'm tired, too.

I want to lie down beside her on the bed.

I want to, but when I look down at our hands, I see the red thread on my wrist, a reminder to come back.

In the bed, Lara's breath hitches, and I don't know if it's sweat or tears running down her face. "They never stay," she whispers.

I look through the hospital window, to the man and woman in the hall, talking frantically with the doctor. I can't hear what they're saying, because Lara never did, but they look upset. They look frightened. Helpless.

But even if they can't help, I can.

I just have to figure out how.

If she were a ghost, I could hold up a mirror. Show her what I see, remind her who she is. But she's not a ghost, not yet, so I'll just have to tell her instead.

"Listen to me, Lara," I say as she curls up smaller on the bed. "You're the smartest person I know, and I need you to teach me, to show me, to save me from all the stupid, reckless decisions I'll make, because Jacob can't."

"Ghost," she whispers, with just a shadow of her normal disdain. But it's a shadow, and I hold on to it.

"Lara Chowdhury, you have to wake up so we can get out of this place. You have to wake up, because if you don't, you never will." My voice cracks. "You have to wake up because you're my friend, and I'm not leaving here without you."

A small furrow appears between her brows. Her eyes drift open, glassy and fevered.

"Cassidy?" she says.

"Yes," I say, the word rushing out.

She blinks, and as she does, she grows up, aging from the small girl in the bed to the one I know. She looks around.

"How did I get here?"

"The Emissary," I say. "The bridge."

Her eyes sharpen, finally coming into focus. "I remember."

Lara tries to get up, but she can't. I help her sit, and then stand, let her lean her weight on me.

"I'm so sorry," I say. "The Emissary was after me, not you, and—"

"Oh, don't bother, Cassidy," she cuts in, sounding more like herself. "We're in-betweeners, after all. Death is an occupational hazard."

I smile, almost laugh, before I notice that the hospital room is getting darker around us, the details dissolving into shadow.

"Cassidy!"

Jacob's voice swims through the room, faint and far away. I help Lara to the door. She grabs the handle, forcing the door open, and we step through. And as we do, the hospital falls away and we're back on the Bridge of Souls, nothing but wind, and mist, and Jacob, looking wide-eyed.

"Hello, Ghost," says Lara, right before Jacob flings his arms around her neck. She staggers a little, but I don't know if it's surprise or the lingering fever, the head-swimming wrongness of this place.

"We have to get out of here," I say.

"Yeah," says Jacob, "about that."

He points over my shoulder. Back, toward the beginning of the bridge. Back toward the land of the living. Back toward safety.

I squint into the mist.

At first, I can't see anything.

And then I see a streak of black.

A broad-brimmed hat, floating in the fog.

And long limbs in a crisp dark suit.

And a bone-white mask with a frozen grin.

The Emissary walks toward us through the mist.

And even though it doesn't have a face, somehow, it still looks very, very mad.

CHAPTER
TWENTY-THREE

Back in the land of the living, the Emissary was a skeletal thing, a thin figure in a skull mask and a dark suit. Something almost human.

Here on the bridge, it doesn't look human at all.

Its once-gloved hands are now bone-white talons, and its broad-brimmed hat is a halo of night, the air around it smudged a charcoal black. Cold and darkness spill off its limbs, and every step it takes leaves an inky stain on the bridge.

And it is coming straight toward us.

"You belong to Death," says the Emissary in a voice like smoke rising from a fire. Like steam hissing from the lid of a pot. *"And we will take you back."*

"I don't think so!" shouts Jacob, flinging himself in

front of me. He looks back over his shoulder, arms spread wide as if he can single-handedly keep the monster at bay.

A smile flickers at the edge of Jacob's mouth. "I can slow it down," he says, turning back to face the Emissary. *"Run."*

Maybe he *can* slow it down.

Maybe he's strong enough to face the Emissary.

Maybe he can buy us time.

But I'm not leaving this place without *both* of my friends. I grab Jacob's wrist and pull him away from the creature. Grab Lara's hand, and together, we run.

The world at our backs is dark, but the road ahead is lighter. If we can just get off the Bridge of Souls. If we can—

"Where are you going?" rasps the Emissary, and there is an awful amusement in that hoarse voice. As if there's nowhere to go, as if the bridge doesn't run both ways.

The Emissary lifts one hand, bone talons pointed toward the sky—if there is a sky in a place like this. And suddenly the bridge beneath us ripples and sways. Thin black ropes shoot up from the ground, reaching for us, wrapping around our ankles and wrists. I twist free of one, dodge another, but the third coils around my calf and the fourth catches me around the stomach. I stumble and fall, hitting the bridge hard. My camera wedges up against my ribs, knocking the air from my lungs, and Lara's red backpack goes skidding several feet away.

It stops near Lara herself. She's on the ground, too, fighting as half a dozen ropes try to pin her down. Jacob alone seems immune to the black threads. He kneels beside me, tearing at the brittle ropes as the Emissary makes its slow way toward us.

I tear free of the last rope, but the monstrous reaper only chuckles.

"You cannot run from us," it says.

And the thing is, I know it's right.

This is a fisherman, and we are the fish. We have to break the line.

"Jacob," I say, lunging for the red backpack in the middle of the bridge. "Get Lara!"

He's already there, at her side, ripping out the ropes like weeds as they climb around her. Instead of running, I unzip the bag and turn out the last of the ingredients from the banishing spell.

The pouch of grave dirt is almost empty.

A few spoonfuls of oil slosh in the bottom of the bottle.

A handful of stones and the box of matches tumble out, and I scramble for them, too.

"Get behind me!" I shout as Jacob pulls Lara to her feet. One braid has come loose, her black hair escaping its plait, and she's breathing heavily, but she's up, and together they hurry toward me.

The Emissary doesn't.

It moves with a terrifying slowness, the steady pace of someone—some*thing*—that knows its prey won't escape. Jacob and Lara sink to their knees beside me. Lara understands what I'm doing. She starts to arrange the stones.

"Will this actually work?" asks Jacob, still ripping out every rope that reaches up through the bridge.

"I have no idea," I say. "I'm making this up as I go."

But I saw the way the spell burned through the layers of the world, from the living realm into the Veil. So maybe, just maybe, it will work here, too.

I can't make a circle. I don't have enough dirt, or oil, and even if I did, the Emissary would never step inside it. A line will have to do. I scatter the last of the grave dirt, little more than a smear against the darkened bridge. Lara pours the oil in a thin line, her hands somehow steady, even now.

I draw a match, before remembering—Jacob. My heart tumbles into my stomach. If I strike the match, if I do the spell, what will happen? Will he be trapped here? Will he be sent on?

There are no right answers, said the fortune-teller. *You cannot win without losing, too.*

Jacob meets my gaze, and smiles.

"It's okay, Cass."

But it's not. I fling my arms around his shoulders. Tears slide down my cheeks. I can't do this. I can't lose my best friend.

"We're running out of time," hisses Lara as the Emissary gets closer.

"No matter what happens," Jacob whispers in my ear, "you'll never lose me."

And then, before I can stop him, he grabs the box of matches and strikes one, dropping the flame onto the oil.

It catches.

And burns.

The fire spreads from the middle out, and the Emissary rears back, away from the smoldering line. Jacob sways, going gray, and I squeeze my hand around his, trying to keep him there, with me, trying to keep our line from breaking.

Shadows flicker across the Emissary's mask. *"We . . . will . . ."* but it can't seem to finish the line. It tips its head, as if trying to remember.

The spell is working.

And then the fire sputters, and goes out.

For a second, I think the spell is done, that it *worked*, even though Jacob is still here. But then I look down and realize, with a growing horror, that the line didn't burn. There wasn't enough oil. The banishing didn't work.

The Emissary smiles, and steps smoothly over the ashes of the broken spell.

Jacob's hand tears free of mine.

He lets out a primal shout and flings himself forward at the Emissary, the way he did before, in the graveyard. There, we were in the land of the living, and Jacob was just a ghost. Here, the Emissary may be something *more*, but so is Jacob.

He slams into the skull-faced figure, pushing him back across the line, inky boots smearing the grave dirt on the bridge. Jacob slams his hands against the Emissary's chest, but this time, instead of stepping back, the Emissary holds its ground, and Jacob's fists sink into its front, like quicksand.

Jacob gasps and tries to pull free, but his arms sink deeper into the black suit. His sneakers slide on the bridge as the Emissary drags him in.

"You are in the wrong place," says the rasping voice. *"We will send you back."*

The color starts to drain out of Jacob's face, his shirt, his hair, his skin. Something inside me begins to tear. A thread unraveling. A connection breaking.

"Cassidy . . ." Jacob says, his voice small and thin. "Go."

I start toward him, but Lara catches my arm.

"We have to go," she says, but I twist free, surging toward my friend, the camera already in my hands. The flash won't work, I know, but the camera's still heavy. I wrap my fingers in the purple strap and swing the camera as hard as I can, right at the Emissary's head.

It hits the bone mask with a sound like metal on stone, like breaking pottery.

The Emissary loses its hold on Jacob.

Jacob collapses onto the bridge, and I don't have time to run to him, to see if he's okay, because the Emissary rounds on me, the ghost forgotten. The rictus grin of the skeleton mask splits and cracks, inky blackness dripping between the broken pieces of the mask.

"Cassidy Blake, your time has come."

It reaches out a gloved hand.

This time, there is no invitation. No quiet order to *come with us.*

It simply drives its hand into my chest.

CHAPTER
TWENTY-FOUR

I look down and see the Emissary's fingers, curling around the thread behind my ribs, the blue-white light of my life flickering in its grip. Darkness swarms over my senses.

My heart stutters, skips a beat.

Out of the corner of my eye, I see Lara, kneeling over Jacob, and I realize, this is the end, and I'm not scared to die again, not like this, protecting my friends.

"We will take you back into the dark."

My vision tunnels. I squeeze my eyes shut. I can't breathe.

"What about me?" Lara's voice is crisp and clear.

I drag my eyes open and see her, standing there, several feet away, the warm red light of her life shining through her chest. The Emissary's grip loosens a little.

"Lara, stop," I whisper.

"*I* fled from Death," she says, the words as strong as

the in-betweener's oath. *Look and listen. See and know.*

"Why don't you come for *me*?"

No.

"*I* fled from Death," I say, and the Emissary's broken face swivels back to me. Its fingers tighten around my life, and I shiver, suddenly cold.

"*I* stole from Death," Lara says, as if it's a contest, a competition. This time, the Emissary lets go. Its taloned hand draws out of my chest, and I slump, dizzy and breathless, to the bridge.

It starts toward Lara. "*We will take you.*"

And despite everything, Lara Chowdhury holds her ground. She doesn't take a single step back. She is the bravest girl I know. And I can't let her do this.

"*I* stole from Death!" I echo, and the Emissary stops halfway between us.

"*We know,*" it says. "*We will take you both.*"

"But who's first?" I ask.

"It should be me," demands Lara.

"No," I say. "You came for me, right?"

"You didn't even notice *me*."

269

The Emissary looks between us, unsure who to take.

Which is why it doesn't see Jacob.

Not until it's too late.

Doesn't notice how close it's standing to the side of the rail-less bridge, until the pale gray streak of my best friend throws himself around its skeletal waist, carrying the darkness with him toward the edge.

And over.

"Jacob!" I shout, diving forward as he vanishes over the side. I get there in time to see the Emissary fall, down, down, down into the bottomless dark. And Jacob, scrambling to hold on to the lip of the bridge, and slipping.

I thrust the purple strap of my broken camera over the edge, feel the sudden snag of weight, like a fish on a line, and look down to see Jacob clutching at it.

"I've got you," I say through gritted teeth. But he's not weightless here, and the force of him drags me forward toward the edge and the bottomless mist below.

But just as I start to slip, Lara reaches me, wraps her arms around my waist, and together, we pull Jacob up out of the dark. We all sprawl, breathless, on the polished black stone.

I crawl to the edge and look down, searching the mist.

There is no sign of the Emissary.

No sound, either, just the silence of the empty dark. And my own pulse, like a warning in my ears, telling me I've been here far too long. Telling me to get off this bridge, and out of the Veil, and back where I belong—in the land of the living.

I get to my feet, and turn to see my friends.

Lara is trying to smooth her shirt, her hands shaking. She looks more disheveled than I've ever seen her. But otherwise, she looks like herself.

Jacob, on the other hand, looks like a *ghost*. He stands there staring out into the mist, thin and pale as a sliver of ice, and I remember the horrible feeling I had when the Emissary had him, like the thing between us was breaking. Like I was losing him.

Jacob, I think, but he doesn't glance over.

"Look at me," I say, catching his face in my hands. "Your name is Jacob Ellis Hale, you have two brothers, you lived and drowned in upstate New York and then you saved my life, and now we're best friends."

He stares straight at me for a long moment, and then

he scrunches up his face. "I know," he says, as if I've lost my mind.

I throw my arms around his shoulders and try not to think about how light he feels, like he's not all there.

"I thought I lost you," I say.

"Rule number eighty-one of friendship," he answers. "Friends don't let friends get murdered by horrifying skull monsters on the bridge between the Veil and the place beyond."

I laugh, and pull back to look at him.

And then I punch him in the shoulder.

"Ow!"

"You don't feel pain," I say.

"Says you," he says, rubbing his arm. "What was that for?"

"You could have died," I snap. *"Again."*

"Yeah, well. It worked, didn't it?"

"If it's all the same to you," says Lara, swinging her red backpack onto her shoulder, "I'd really like to get out of here."

"Agreed," says Jacob.

"Yeah," I chime in. Even without the Emissary, the Bridge of Souls is not a friendly place.

We start back, side by side, Jacob recounting our adventure like a highlight reel, telling Lara about the hearse and the river before diving into the parts she was there for. It feels like we walked so far. But going back the other way, the bridge is short. Soon the mist clears, and the edge of the lake comes into sight. We step off the bridge, back into the pale gray landscape of the Veil, the space flat and blank as paper.

I'm already reaching for the curtain of the Veil, already dreaming of solid ground and a hot shower, and a long night's sleep, when Jacob clears his throat.

"Hey," he says. "Um, I think something's wrong."

I look back over my shoulder. "What?"

Jacob reaches out, as if for the Veil, opens and closes his hand, but there's nothing there. His fingers fall back to his side.

"I don't think I can . . ."

"Of course you can," I say. When Jacob pulled me out of the land of the living, I pulled him out of the land of the dead. As long as I've known him, he's been able to move between our world and the Veil. That's how he can exist so far from the place where he drowned. That's how he can haunt me, wherever I go.

"Take my hand," I say.

He does, and I try to ignore how fragile his fingers feel—not so much skin and bone as humid air—as I reach for the curtain. But it doesn't work. I can feel the Veil, waiting, but when I try to pull it aside and step through, Jacob's hand slips from mine, turns to nothing. Like he's not even there.

"It's okay," he says, his voice tight.

But it's not okay.

I turn toward Lara, who's been looking carefully away. As if she knew this would happen.

"You always said that Jacob and I were tangled up, and that's why he was getting stronger," I say to her. "So something came untangled back there on the bridge. How do I fix it?"

"Cassidy," she says softly. "Maybe it *is* fixed."

"Then help me unfix it!"

"Cass," starts Jacob, "we knew this might—"

"*No,*" I snap, turning on him. "I almost lost you twice, and I'm not doing it again. I'm not saying goodbye. I shouldn't have to." I jab him in the chest. "We fought Death, and we won. So *no*, I'm not giving up on you. You're Jacob Ellis Hale, you're not like other ghosts, and you don't belong in the Veil. You belong with me. And I'm not going home without you. Understand?"

Jacob nods.

I squeeze his hand, as tight as I can, as if I can pour some of my life back into him. I imagine the blue-white light inside my chest spreading down my arm and through my fingers, wrapping around Jacob's like a rope.

He brightens a little, a tiny bit of color slipping back into his clothes, his skin.

And something inside me breaks, because I know it's not enough.

He's still too ghostly, too gray.

And then Lara reaches out and takes his other hand.

"Come on, Ghost," she says, squeezing tight. I can almost see the red light of her life, spreading down her fingers and into his. I can only hope it will be enough.

I take a deep breath and reach for the Veil again. And this time, I feel the gray cloth catch in my hand. I grab the curtain tight, and pull it aside.

And hand in hand in hand, we take a step, and fall.

CHAPTER TWENTY-FIVE

The sun is going down over New Orleans.

Philippa leans against the hood of the hearse, plucking petals from a flower stolen off the funeral wreath. Lucas sits in the passenger seat, reading a book.

I look down at my hand, where Jacob's fingers were tight in mine, but it's empty. I look over at Lara, and Jacob, who's supposed to be between us, but he's not.

It didn't work.

Sadness washes over Lara's face, and she pulls me into a hug.

"I'm sorry," she says softly. "I'm so—"

And then we hear a voice a couple of feet behind us.

"This sucks."

Lara and I both turn to see Jacob standing there, the Causeway at his back.

I let out a sound, half laugh and half sob and all relief, wishing I could throw my arms around him. But Jacob doesn't even seem to notice. He's too busy staring down at his hands, his face contorted in annoyance. And I realize why.

I can see him.

But I can also see *through* him.

I didn't notice how solid he was getting before, until I see him like this. His colors washed thin, his skin between pale and gray. He was like this in the beginning, when he first started haunting me. When I looked up from my hospital bed and saw him sitting, cross-legged, in the visitor's chair.

When he followed me home.

A ghost.

And nothing more.

But of course, Jacob is so much more. And he's *here*, and that's all that matters. He sighs. "Oh well." And I wish I could hit him, or hug him, but I settle for a ghost five.

"Ah, there you are!" says Philippa, tossing away the remains of the flower as we return to the hearse.

"Cassidy, Lara," says Lucas, climbing out of the car, his expression full of deep relief.

"Nice to see you all alive," says Philippa. "Well," she adds, nodding at Jacob, "you know what I mean." She squints, studying him. "You are looking a bit thin, aren't you?"

"You should see the other guy," he says.

"Hah!" chimes Philippa. "I love a funny ghost. Now, tell me everything! How did it go? What was it like?"

Another car slows at the sight of a man, a woman, two girls, and a hearse on the side of the road.

"Perhaps we can talk on the way?" says Lucas.

Philippa sighs. "Fine, fine, but you better not leave anything out."

She doesn't need to drive as fast on the way back. No one's life is on the line. Time isn't of the essence. But that doesn't stop Philippa from swerving through rush hour traffic.

Lucas braces his hands on the dash. Jacob and I slide more than once. Lara grips the side door and grimaces. I guess the horseless carriage was a smoother ride.

"Philippa," she says, looking over her shoulder. "You do know there's a coffin in the back seat."

"That's Fred," Jacob and I answer at the same time.

"Excellent," says Lara, as if that answers everything.

By the time the hearse rolls through the French Quarter and pulls up in front of the Hotel Kardec, we've told

Philippa and Lucas everything. Lucas makes notes in his book, but says we'll have to tell Renée or Michael so they can make a proper record of what we've seen and learned.

"For the next time it happens," he says.

"Next time?" yelps Jacob. "No thank you."

And for once, I'm in complete agreement. I've had enough Emissaries and bridges to last me a good long while.

Lucas, Jacob, and I climb out of the hearse, but when I turn, I see Lara's still inside.

"You coming?"

She shakes her head. "I think your parents would get a bit suspicious," she says, "if I stayed a second night. Philippa's offered to let me sleep at her place."

"It will be fun," says Philippa. "Amethyst loves company. Byron, not so much."

"Is Byron your boyfriend?" I ask, and Philippa cackles.

"No, he's my snake."

Lara makes a panicked face.

"You sure you don't want to stay with me?" I ask.

She swallows and shakes her head. "No, it will be fine."

A car honks for the hearse to move on.

"How rude!" says Philippa. "The living have no respect

for the dead." She puts the car into gear. "Sleep sweet!" she calls, and with that, they're gone.

Lucas turns to me. "Will you be all right?" he asks.

I swallow and nod. "I think so," I say. "At least for now."

Lucas flashes a quiet smile. "If history teaches us anything," he says, "it's how to live in the present."

Jacob and I say goodbye to Lucas, and we go inside the hotel, across the lobby with the still-closed séance room. As we head upstairs, I brace for one of Mom and Dad's lectures about staying out too long, or wandering too far. So I'm startled when I open the hotel door and find the room quiet and dark.

They're not back yet.

"Whew," says Jacob.

Grim looks up at me, green eyes wide, and for a moment, I wonder if he was worried. But then he walks over to his food bowl, and I think he might just be hungry. I'm kneeling down to feed him when the hotel door unlocks, and Mom and Dad sweep through.

"And so I was saying—oh, Cassidy! You're back. How was—" Mom stops talking because I've flung myself into her arms, tears pricking my eyes.

"Cass," says Dad, joining the hug. "What's wrong?"

I almost died today, I think. *I almost lost my best friends in the world beyond the Veil. It was terrifying, and awful, and I survived.* And I can't tell them any of that, so I just shake my head against them both.

"Nothing," I say. "Nothing at all. I just missed you."

Mom hugs me tight. "Are you hungry?"

"No," I say. "Just tired."

She pulls back to study my face, and shakes her head.

"Honestly, Cassidy," she says, wiping at my cheek, "how do you always get so filthy?"

I look down at myself.

"Let's see," says Jacob, ticking the reasons off on his fingers. "A failed spell, a run through the Quarter, a ride in a hearse, and a battle on a bridge . . ."

"What happened to your camera?" asks Dad, horrified.

I wince, afraid to look down. I heard the crack, and the crunch, of course, but I hadn't wanted to see how bad it was.

Turns out, it's pretty bad.

The lens is shot through with cracks. The back has broken open, ruining the film. One corner has been badly dented where it struck the Emissary's mask. The purple strap is fraying, the place where Jacob held on marked by his fingers, the violet faded almost to gray.

"I fell down," I say, wishing I had a better answer, but the truth probably wouldn't go over very well.

"Are you sure you're all right?" asks Dad, clearly more worried about me than my poor camera.

I take a deep breath. "I am now." I clutch the broken camera. It's been with me through so much.

"It's okay, Cass," says Dad, pulling me close. "Things can be repaired. People are harder to fix."

"Tell me about it," says Jacob, sprawling on the floor near the open comic he's been reading. He tries to turn the pages, but nothing happens. Not so much as a breeze. He groans, and rolls onto his back. Grim pads over and stretches out next to him, purring softly in sympathy.

"Well, filming's done," says Mom. "And we still have a full day. What shall we do tomorrow?"

"We could go for a drive," offers Dad, "across the Causeway br—"

"No!" Jacob and I shout at the same time, but of course, they only hear me.

Dad holds up his hands. "It was just a suggestion. What would *you* like to do, Cass?"

I think long and hard, and then say, "I vote for beignets."

"That's my girl," says Mom with a grin.

My parents sit down to go through the footage, and I take a very, very long shower, trying to rinse the Veil and the Bridge of Souls from my skin. Afterward, I fall into bed, so tired that when sleep folds over me, I drop straight down, and don't even dream.

CHAPTER TWENTY-SIX

The beignets are just as good the second time.

We sit around the table at Café du Monde, Mom chatting with Jenna and Adan about the footage, Dad deep in conversation with Lucas about the history of the church in the square. Meanwhile, I'm locked in battle with a beignet, determined not to spill sugar on my jeans as I eat, while Jacob sulks because he can't for the life—or death—of him move the tiny mountain of powdered sugar on top of the fried dough.

"Give me time," he says, frowning in concentration. "I'll get it."

I'm sure he will eventually, but for now, he's taken a step back on the material front. He's definitely become more transparent since the bridge.

"Trans*lucent*," he corrects me sulkily. "They're not the same thing."

And more sensitive, I add.

The truth is, it's kind of nice, not having to worry about your best friend becoming a powerful, potentially unstable spirit, at least for today.

We're on our second order of beignets when Lara shows up, Philippa in tow.

Lucas's eyes widen. Philippa looks a little surprised, too, but it's more of a happy surprise, like waking up to pancakes. Or beignets.

"This is my aunt Philly," says Lara, and I almost laugh.

Lara and Philippa could not possibly be more different. Lara's prim, straight-backed, and all adult attitude in a kid's body. Philippa, on the other hand, is like Luna Lovegood in a grown-up's shell. Cheerful, whimsical, and not entirely there. She's wearing a tie-dyed blue-and-white dress that looks like a giant version of the evil eye, and a pair of neon-orange sunglasses.

Mom looks between them, a bit skeptical, and I can't blame her.

They certainly don't *look* related. Lara's glossy black hair and light brown skin versus Philippa's white-blond wave and skin so pale, she looks more like a ghost than a person.

"Rude," says Jacob.

"You're awfully young to be Lara's aunt," says Mom.

"I know, right?" says Philippa, as if she's just as confused.

"We're really more like cousins twice removed," explains Lara, shooting the Society psychic a meaningful look.

A look Philippa clearly misses because she says, "We're not even actually related. I'm just the daughter of someone who married someone . . ." She waves her hand as if the rest doesn't matter.

"You two must be close, though," says Dad. "For Lara to come all this way."

"We are," says Lara, but she looks at me when she says it, and I feel this warm energy in my chest, right where the ribbon glows. Because she did come a very long way for a friend.

"Oh, beignets!" says Philippa, and she doesn't even get the pastry to her mouth before spilling half the sugar down her dress. Not that she seems to care.

Philippa and Lara pull up two more chairs and gather round, and even though it's a motley group—two paranormal investigators, a two-person camera crew, two members of the Society, two in-betweeners, and a ghost—for a little while, we're just a group of people, sharing pastry and stories.

At some point, Lara and I exchange a look. The grown-ups are going over show notes and postproduction, and I grab her hand and get up.

"We're going to take a walk," I say, pulling her into the sun, Jacob on our heels.

"Don't go far," warns Mom.

"We'll stay in the square," I say.

The sun is scorching and bright as we make our way, hopping between puddles of shade.

"I wish I didn't have to go back," Lara says softly. "One upside: Philippa took me by the Society this morning, and they finally agreed to make me a member."

"That's amazing!" I say.

"Well, honorary member, until I turn sixteen. But I'll work on that. As I explained to Renée, death doesn't discriminate between young and old, so why should they? So what if I'm twelve?"

"You're not exactly a normal twelve-year-old," says Jacob, and I'm not sure if he meant it as a compliment, but Lara smiles.

"Why, thank you." Her smile flickers and fades. "There's a lot they don't know, a lot I plan to help them learn, about us, and about that . . . place yesterday." She shivers a little. "I felt so helpless."

"But you weren't," I say. "You fought with us, on the bridge. You distracted the Emissary."

"After you saved me," she says. "If you hadn't been there, in the hospital, I'm not sure I would have . . ."

I squeeze her hand. "But you did."

Lara sighs heavily. "Being an in-betweener used to be so straightforward. And don't get me wrong, I *do* love a challenge, but sometimes I miss the simple satisfaction of hunting ghosts. No offense, Jacob," she adds.

"None taken," he says, scuffing his shoe.

The Veil ripples around us, carrying a wave of smoke and jazz, and I know the perfect parting gift for Lara Chowdhury.

"Hey," I say. "Do you want to catch a serial killer?"

Lara's dark eyebrows rise. And then she smiles. "Why not?"

"Well, that's better," says Jacob when we step through the Veil.

He looks down at himself, clearly relieved that he's a bit more solid on this side of the curtain.

Around us, Jackson Square is a tangle of fire and sunshine, shouting and song. And the more time I spend in New Orleans, the more I realize it fits, this strange, chaotic melody.

Speaking of melodies, I listen, picking up the strain of music. I follow it around carriages and through crowds to the jazz band playing in the corner of the square.

And there he is, leaning up against that same post, hat tipped down and an axe on his shoulder. The nice thing about ghosts in the Veil is that they tend to be pretty consistent, acting out the same loop over and over.

"The Axeman of New Orleans," says Lara brightly. "What a treat. You know he was never caught? Though I suppose here in the Veil, the axe kind of gives him away."

"Your excitement is a little creepy," says Jacob, but Lara's already starting forward, her mirror pendant ready in her hand.

Jacob and I run after her.

"Excuse me, sir," she says, stopping just out of swinging range.

The Axeman's gaze flicks from the band toward Lara, clearly annoyed at the interruption.

"Can't you see I'm listening?" he mutters.

"Oh, I can see that," she says. "But can't *you* see I have a job to do?"

She lifts the mirror.

"Look and listen," she starts, but the Axeman must not have been looking straight at her, because he catches the first glint of light and smells trouble. He swings a hand up to shield his eyes, already turning away.

But that's where I am, Mom's compact mirror in my palm.

"See and know," I say, and he shudders to a stop, face contorted.

"This is what you are," we say at the same time, and something in the Axeman switches off like a light. All the color leaches from him, and his edges ripple and thin, and all I have to do is reach in and take the thread.

But this one's for Lara, so I nod at her and say, "Go ahead."

"You can do it," she says, and I shrug and step forward, reaching toward the ghost's chest when Jacob says, "Wait!"

We both turn toward him, and he bounces on his toes, looking both eager and nervous. "Can *I* do it?"

Lara and I exchange a look. Understandably, Jacob has never been very supportive of the ghost-hunting part of my life.

"Are you sure?" I ask.

Jacob's head bobs. "I mean, if you insist on hunting down ghosts and sending them on, it feels like I should get to do something, and since I don't have a mirror, the pulling-out-the-string bit is really the only one I can do."

"Sure," says Lara.

"Go on," I add.

Jacob approaches the Axeman. He cracks his knuckles and stretches. Lara rolls her eyes, and I smile. And then Jacob takes a deep breath and plunges his hand into the Axeman's chest. He makes a face, as if the ghost were a bowl of peeled grapes on Halloween, a mound of cold spaghetti. Jacob roots around inside the Axeman's chest before he catches hold of the thread, and pulls it out.

It comes free, gray and crumbling, and Jacob promptly drops it on the ground, where it collapses into ash.

"Eww," Jacob says, shaking out his fingers. "*So* gross."

Lara and I only laugh as the Axeman fades and disappears. It feels good, getting back to normal. Or at least, our version of it.

We cross back through the Veil, a brief moment of cold, quickly replaced by summer sun.

Jacob looks down at himself and sighs, clearly disappointed by his transparency.

"Translucency," he mutters as we make our way back across the square.

But when Café du Monde comes into sight, I slow down.

"Lara," I say, afraid to ask, "we killed the Emissary, right?"

I mean, it went over the side of the bridge. We saw it fall. There was no place below, nothing but mist. And yet, I'm not surprised when Lara shakes his head.

"I don't think you can kill something like that," she says. "I don't think they can die."

I bite my lip. "But it's gone, right? I mean, it's not still coming after us."

"Yes," she says, "according to Renée, that one should be gone."

"That one," I echo.

She sighs, turning toward me. "I don't think it's a one-time thing, Cassidy. Eventually, another Emissary will notice you. Or me. Eventually, it will come back and try again. That's what Death does." I sag a little at the thought, feeling hopeless. But Lara doesn't seem discouraged, only determined. "That's what it means to be alive. Every day, whether you're a regular person or an in-betweener. You run as long as you can, but Death always catches up."

Jacob shivers. "Great pep talk."

But Lara shakes her head. "I've never met anyone who outran Death forever. And I've never met anyone who truly wanted to." She takes me by the shoulders. "So yes, Death will come for us again, one way or another. We can't live in fear of it. That's no way to live at all."

CHAPTER
TWENTY-SEVEN

When we get back to the café, the plates have been cleared, the bill paid. Everyone is packing up, as if ready to go. Jenna and Adan are the first to leave. Adan ruffles my hair and offers a rare smile. Jenna unhooks one of the many chains around her neck and offers it to me. The charm on the end is a tiny silver skull.

"Something to remember New Orleans by," she says, as if I could possibly forget.

They wave, and wish us luck, and then the pair drift away across the square.

Philippa looks around cheerfully.

"Any plans for the day?" she asks. "We've got all the time in the world."

Lara clears her throat. "Aunt Philly," she says. "I have a flight to catch, *remember*?"

"Oh yes, that . . ." Philippa looks at her wrist, even though she's not wearing a watch. "Your parents, the plane, of course. We should be going?" The sentence ticks up at the end, into a question.

Lara sighs. "Yes, I think we have to."

"Well then," she says. "I'll get the hearse."

Mom and Dad straighten a little. Each clearly has their own questions about that statement, and each decides not to ask.

"I'm sorry we took so much of your niece's time," says Mom.

Philippa looks surprised. "Niece?"

Lara squeezes Philippa's hand *very* tightly. "Oh, yes, well, I got to see plenty of her. And I'm sure she'll come back, now that she's a memb—"

Lara coughs. Lucas glares at Philippa, who realizes, a little late, that she's about to reveal their secret society to a pair of paranormal investigators.

She changes course. "Now that she knows she's always welcome here."

Lucas sighs audibly.

Lara turns to me. "Well, Cassidy," she starts, and I

swear, her eyes are a little glossy. "I suppose, for now at least, this is—"

I throw my arms around her.

Lara stumbles a little, under the sudden force of the hug.

Jacob joins in, and she groans and mutters, "Shove off, Ghost," too soft for anyone else to hear.

"Be safe," I say.

"Be smart," she answers.

She shoots Jacob a look. "And try to stay out of trouble."

And then, too soon, she's walking away. A perfect black braid and a bright red backpack vanishing into the crowd.

I watch her go, wondering when we'll cross paths again, how long it will be before—

My cell phone dings, and I tap it to find a text.

> Lara:
> Rule number fifty-four of friendship: stay in touch.

I smile and write back.

> Me:
> I'll miss you, too.

Mom and Dad head into the café to use the restrooms, and Lucas and I sit in silence, while Jacob tries and fails to move the sugar on the table.

And then the Society's historian sits forward.

"I almost forgot," he says, reaching into his pocket. "Renée wanted you to have this." He holds out a business card, black on black, so that I can only see the symbol of the Society when it catches the light. "In case of trouble."

He reaches into his other pocket. "And Michael sent along this," he says, handing me a white velvet pouch. Tiny beads rattle inside.

"In case of trouble," he says again, and I tip the beads into my palm, and see that each and every one is marked by the black and blue and white circles of the evil eye.

"And this," says Lucas, holding out a tiny box, "is from me."

I open the box. Inside is a sturdy leather cord with a brand-new mirror pendant hanging on the end, its surface polished to a shine.

"It's perfect," I say, looping the cord around my neck and tucking the mirror under my shirt. The moment it settles there, I feel better. Like I've been balancing on one foot, and now both are safely on the ground. "Thank you, Lucas."

My parents come back to the table.

"And you, Professor Dumont?" asks Mom. "Must we say goodbye to you?"

Lucas smiles and rises to his feet, not a speck of sugar on him. "I'm afraid so."

He shakes Mom's hand, and Dad's, and then mine, and strolls away in the direction of Thread & Bone.

Mom, Dad, Jacob, and I set off across Jackson Square, passing musicians with open cases, and people selling charms, a woman in white, standing still as a statue, and—

"Care to have your fortune told?"

I turn and see a man with a folding table, a stack of tarot cards facedown on top.

"The first one's free," he adds.

And I'd be lying if I said I wasn't at least a little curious, if my fingers didn't twitch toward the cards the way they do toward the Veil, half scared and half excited to see what's on the other side.

But there's no way to know what the future holds, and even if there were, I wouldn't want to know.

"No thanks," I say, shaking my head.

Mom and Dad glance back, wondering where I've gone, but I catch up, and we set off, two parents, a girl, and a ghost.

Dad holds my hand, and Mom swings her arm around my shoulders, and Jacob runs up ahead, dodging between tourists.

The French Quarter is messy and bright around us, a tangle of music and laughter, the here and the Veil, the living and the dead. And I know the future is uncertain, and that Death comes for everyone. But as I walk between summer sun and brief bits of shade, I feel lighter than I have in ages. Who knows what waits beyond the Veil.

Right now, I'm just glad to be alive.

When Cass's family head off to Edinburgh, Cass meets a girl who shares her "gift" of entering the world of the spirits. Cass still has a lot to learn about the Veil – and herself. And fast...

A thrillingly spooky and action-packed tale of hauntings, history, mystery and the bond between friends (even if that friend is a ghost...)

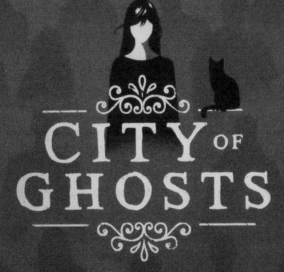

A haunted girl.
An adventure like no other.

CITY OF
GHOSTS

NEW YORK TIMES BESTSELLING AUTHOR

VICTORIA SCHWAB

Cass is in Paris, where her parents are filming their TV show about the world's most haunted cities. When Cass accidentally awakens a frighteningly strong spirit in the creepy underground Catacombs, she must rely on her still-growing skills as a ghosthunter – and turn to friends both old and new to help her unravel a mystery.

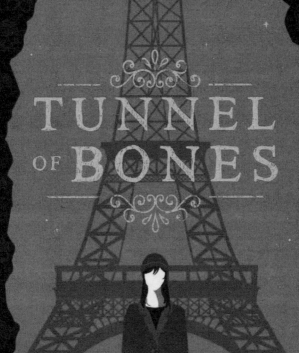

VICTORIA SCHWAB

TUNNEL OF BONES

Aria is a guardian angel. She can use her shadow like a door, to travel from place to place. She can dream things into existence. And she can see when certain people need help. She must find and guide three girls – Gabby, Caroline and Mikayla – through each of their problems to earn her wings. But helping these girls is no easy feat – even for someone with magical powers. Still, she's up for the challenge...

Three enchanting novels in one irresistible volume.

ABOUT THE AUTHOR

Victoria (V. E.) Schwab is the #1 *New York Times* bestselling author of more than a dozen novels for young adults and adults, including the Shades of Magic series, *Vicious*, *Vengeful*, *This Savage Song*, and *Our Dark Duet*. Victoria lives in Nashville, Tennessee, but she can often be found haunting Paris streets and trudging up Scottish hillsides. Usually, she's tucked in the corner of a coffee shop, dreaming up stories. Visit her online at veschwab.com.